NINER

NINER

Theresa Martin Golding

FRONT STREET
Asheville, North Carolina

Copyright © 2008 by Theresa Martin Golding
All rights reserved
Printed in the United States of America
Designed by Helen Robinson
First edition

Library of Congress Cataloging-in-Publication Data
Golding, Theresa Martin.
Niner / Theresa Martin Golding. — 1st ed.
p. cm.
Summary: When twelve-year-old Macey discovers
a locket on her front steps, she begins a journey
to find out about who she really is and why her
adoptive mother has been gone for almost a year.
ISBN-13: 978-1-59078-549-2 (hardcover : alk. paper)
[1. Adoption—Fiction. 2. Identity—Fiction.] I. Title.
PZ7.G56775Ni 2008
[Fic]—dc22
2007023461

Front Street
An Imprint of Boyds Mills Press, Inc.
815 Church Street
Honesdale, Pennsylvania 18431

To Joe and Pam, with special thanks to Meg and Ty

NINER

1

This was my first funeral, and I was pretty sure I was going to throw up in the pew, right next to the B-O-D-Y. My stomach lurched, like a half-dead animal was in there trying to jump out. I swallowed it back down and tried to ignore the priest on the altar. He was nodding at me with his solemn face and winking, which was my cue to go up and do the second reading, but I didn't move. I couldn't do it, so I stared at my lap, at my folded hands, at my nine fingers, and wondered if I would get my missing thumb back if I made it to heaven. Was there a storage spot up there for all the things that people lost when they were on earth? I pictured my thumb floating on the lost-and-found cloud. If I made it to heaven, which I have to admit was a real long shot, maybe I could finally be perfect, with all the pieces of me fitting together just the right way. I wondered which family I would belong to in heaven. If I were perfect, maybe they would all want me instead of the other way around.

The priest stood up and cleared his throat rather loudly into the microphone. If he were closer, I could have told him what was going on with my stomach. That smelly incense he had shaken all around the C-O-F-F-I-N earlier wasn't helping the situation. The smoke had glided right off the shiny lid and settled on me instead, like my own personal cloud. Even after it disappeared, the sharp smell was stuck inside my nostrils and in the back of my throat. But at least it had gotten me and not Deena. I glanced over at her, worried, but she was staring straight ahead like you're supposed to, and she seemed to be breathing fine.

The priest probably thought I was stupid. He had told me about five times before the Mass started that I was supposed to go up right after Deena, and here I was still glued to the pew. I wish I could be like Deena. She's smart and perfect and not afraid of anything. When it was her turn to read, she had marched confidently to the altar and climbed up on a stool behind the podium. Even with the stool, you could see her only from the chin up—smooth and pimple-free face, shiny blond hair, not a strand out of place. She reached up and pulled the microphone as low as it would go, then read perfectly, looking up at us after every sentence. And she had the hard reading, the one with words like Ephesians and Philippians that I didn't even know what they were.

"This is the word of the Lord," Deena had said.

"Thanks be to God," everyone answered. Except me. I was too nauseous to open my mouth. And I wasn't feeling very thankful either.

The thought had crossed my mind that maybe God wasn't too happy to see me here—in His house—and this pain in my stomach was a punishment for my part in the whole thing. I had had so many chances to change things, but I didn't take any of them. Not one. I gripped the edge of the pew with my sweaty hands and concentrated hard on keeping everything inside.

The priest sighed into the microphone. I ignored him. I desperately tried to keep my thoughts off my stomach. I was wondering what color you get to be in Heaven. I would want to be golden with pure white wings. I had a statue of an angel that looked like that once. Although, I don't want to stick out in heaven the way I do here on earth. Maybe I'd be the same color as everybody else. I'd want to be the same color as Dad.

The priest made a final attempt to get my attention. "The second reading, *please?*" His voice rumbled around the church like a minor earthquake. Goosebumps ran up my arms and down my back.

It felt like the priest was staring at me for an hour, but I guess it was more like a minute. Deena had been poking me the whole time, and I had been inching away from her. Finally, she gave me a hard jab with her elbow. "Macey," she hissed, "it's your turn!"

I wanted to say, "I can't. You do it for me," but I was afraid of what would come out if I opened my mouth.

All those saints with sad-looking faces stared down at me from their stained-glass windows, waiting. Please God, let them leave me alone. I wondered if God could hear prayers better in church than He could at other places. Maybe prayers in church were sort of FedExed to God, and prayers said in your bedroom had to go by regular heavenly mail. The priest finally gave up on me and went on with the service.

I'm ashamed to say that I didn't listen. Maybe more is missing from me besides my thumb. My birth mother must have known it as soon as I was born. Sometimes I imagine the look on her face when she first saw me. Maybe I was like the present that she had always wanted, but when I came, I was broken, missing pieces, incomplete, a rip-off, ugly. So she got rid of me. I can't blame her, really. Maybe I would have done the same thing. I had two foster mothers who I don't remember and then I was adopted when I was about six months old. My mom who adopted me is away, though. That's what I tell everybody because I'm not sure what else to say. Last time I saw her she was waving to me from the bus window, and I don't know where she is anymore. I'm the only person I know who's had four mothers, and not one of them is left.

And I wondered again about the reason for that. What was wrong with me? I used to sometimes imagine my birth parents' genes bubbling deep within me, like mysterious creatures in a murky swamp. When I was overcome with flashes of anger and ugly black thoughts, I worried that those creatures were popping to the surface and grabbing hold of me, dragging me down with them.

I couldn't take any more of this funeral stuff. Somebody should have warned me about all the sad music and the guys in the black suits. And I never would have come if they had told me that the C-O-F-F-I-N would be here, too. It was in the aisle, right next to me. Every time I pictured what was inside it, my stomach lurched and I tasted throw-up in the back of my mouth. I didn't know how much longer I could hold it in.

"I'll be right back," I whispered to Deena through clenched teeth, and slipped out of the pew before she could stop me. The stained-glass saints watched me with their suspicious eyes. They knew I wasn't coming back.

Outside, the sunlight hit me hard as a slap. I leaned over the rail and my stomach clenched and heaved, launching a spray of throw-up all over the azalea bushes below. I felt bad about it, but at least I didn't do it in the pew. I had to keep still for a minute until my legs stopped shaking. I usually like standing here at this high railing because I can see the rooftops of at least a thousand Philadelphia row houses. They seem to run forever, line after straight line, with asphalt streets between them. But today there was no time for sightseeing. I had to get away quickly. I was worried that somebody might come out of the church looking for me. Also, that hearse was sitting at the curb with its blinkers on, and another one of those guys with a black suit was leaning against a black car, staring at me.

When I die, I want to special-order an orange hearse because it's my favorite color and the black one is too sad. I tried to picture my funeral, but I couldn't imagine anyone who would be there besides Deena and Dad. Maybe Mrs. Kennedy, my third-grade teacher, because she was always nice to me. I wondered if Mom or my birth mother would come. One time when I was in school I got a terrible feeling all of a sudden that something was wrong with Deena. Later that day Dad picked me up and told me that Deena had had a bad asthma attack and had to stay in the hospital for a little while.

So maybe my mothers would feel a tingle inside them if I died and know that something had happened. But maybe not.

I hurried away from the church and managed to cross the first six lanes of the boulevard before the light turned red.

"Hey, Niner, nice dress!" Ryan called.

I ignored him. A bunch of the guys were playing football in the grassy median strip. Mom used to hate how the kids played between the lanes and she never knew that sometimes I was one of them. The median is almost as wide as a football field, and when the game is good, we hardly notice the traffic on either side. Besides, it's practically the only green spot in our whole neighborhood.

"Niner! Want to play with us?" Ryan asked.

I stared at the passing cars. I know I didn't tell Ryan everything and it wasn't his fault, but why didn't he go to the church? I wondered if he would go to my funeral, but I doubted it.

Zach sure wouldn't. He'd probably host a party to celebrate my death. He is Ryan's twin, but Zach is shorter and darker and has small, mean eyes. An evil thought slid into my brain before I could stop it—Zach in the C-O-F-F-I-N instead. Wouldn't that have been more fair? I felt myself wishing it and tried hard to think of something else. But the black, ugly thought had a grip on me.

"C'mon. Don't you want to catch a pass, Niner?" Zach called, snickering. He tossed the ball in the air and let it hit him in the head. He fell to the ground and faked a girl scream, kicking his legs. Some of the guys laughed. Ryan looked down at his shoes.

It's hard to catch a football when you're missing a thumb.

I play sometimes, but the ball usually goes through my hands and hits me in the nose or the stomach. I looked at Zach twisting around on the ground, but I didn't say anything. It wasn't worth it. I kept my eye on him, though, because Zach needed to hurt me. He wouldn't be able to stand it until he got me back for what I had done to him. I didn't think he would do it when Ryan was around, but Zach was crazy. You never knew with him.

The light turned green and I crossed the next six lanes. Cars were idling at the red light in the steamy heat and I scanned the faces of the people inside. Deena thinks I'm weird, but I like to come here sometimes just to watch the traffic. I have two reasons. First, it's fun to imagine where all those hundreds of cars are going. Second, I like to look at the people in the cars. You see the weirdest things sometimes: fights, people talking to themselves, dogs in the driver's seat. It's like seeing only the middle of a movie. Then I can make up my own beginning and imagine what happens in the end.

Mostly, though—and I don't tell Deena this because she would get mad—I keep hoping that one day my birth mother will look out her car window and see me. She would recognize me because we probably look alike, only I bet that she's really pretty. She would stop her car, right in the middle of traffic, and get out to meet me. Then I imagine what it would feel like to hug her and have her arms around me. And she would tell me how sorry she was about everything that happened. I wonder if she ever thinks about me or wishes that she didn't give me away. I wonder what kind of person she is.

The light turned and the cars roared off. I took a quick glance back at the church. So far, nobody had come out looking for me. On the median, Ryan poked his head out of the huddle and gave me a little guilty wave. I ignored him again, even though I wished he would leave the game and walk home with me. Sometimes he holds my hand when we walk. It feels good even though he never touches my left hand. Four fingers make a lot of people squeamish.

I dragged myself toward Delaney Street. My shoes hurt, my dress was itchy, and my whole body was clammy with sweat. But I felt worse inside. I climbed up and sat on the sixth step outside my empty house and held my arm up against my chest. The space where my thumb should be was aching. Deena never believes me when I tell her that. "Things that aren't there can't hurt you," she always says. But they do. And I should know.

I was sitting right here on the sixth step that day when I found it. If only I had shared with Deena right away, maybe none of this would have happened.

2

That morning Deena was still asleep, her mouth open and her arm curled around Jake, an old stuffed dog with a brown patch under its eye. Her bangs were damp with sweat and plastered to her forehead. I slipped out of bed and stood in front of the oscillating fan for a minute. Then I threw on a pair of shorts and a T-shirt and went outside for some air.

It was lying there in the grass, plain as day, beside the step where I always sit. I was sure it had to be some kind of message meant just for me. I picked it up and turned it over and over in my hands, a glimmer of excitement dancing inside my stomach. I dreamed of what it could mean.

After a while, the screen door slammed and Deena plopped down beside me, still in her pajamas. "What d'you got?" she asked. "Did you find something?"

I closed my hand real quick. "Oh, it's nothing," I lied.

Deena made a face at me, the scary one where her nostrils get real wide and her lips disappear. "I always share with you," she pouted.

It's true, she does. And Deena always finds the best things, like the Japanese coin and the miniature doll with long, silky hair. Once she even found a twenty-dollar bill. We both went up to Mick's that day and had ice-cream sundaes with the works. Mick gave us each an extra scoop for free, and Deena left him a three-dollar tip. We kept the change for emergencies and put it in the box where we save all the worthwhile stuff that we've found.

But still, even though I finally found something good that I could share with Deena, I couldn't open my fist. If I did, all my excitement and hope would disappear. It was already leaking out between my fingers with Deena sitting beside me. She knows I search for clues every day and she thinks that I'm plain crazy. If I showed her what I had, she would roll her eyes and tell me that it had nothing to do with Mom. Deena's a lot smarter than me, but sometimes I get a certain feeling and I just know things.

"Come on, Macey," Deena whined. "What is it?"

I stuffed my fist down into my pocket. "Let's clean up first," I said. "I promise I'll show you later. Okay?"

We live in the corner row house on Delaney Street, right where the 78 bus stops on its way to Center City. We have a small, flat rectangle of weeds and grass out front and a four-foot stone wall that separates it from the sidewalk. When people are waiting for the bus to come, they sit on our wall and on our front steps. "Next thing you know, they'll be coming inside and asking what's for dinner," Mom used to say. She didn't really mind about the people spreading out in front of our house, but she sure hated how they left all their trash behind. She made a sign once that said Please Don't

Litter—Thank You So Much. Mom was always very polite. Deena and I helped out by painting little flowers all around the sides, and then we staked the sign in the lawn. Somebody stole it the next day.

Deena and I have had the job of cleaning up the litter for years now. Mom used to remind us to do it every day. She's been gone ten months, but we're still at it. When she comes back, we want everything to look real nice. At least, that's why I do it. Deena stopped believing she'd come back when we didn't get a card at Christmas, but I still have hope. Deena and I used to race each other for the mail every day when we heard it slip through the slot in our front door. Sometimes we wrestled for it, rolling around on the floor and even laughing. I always won. Even though I have only nine fingers, I am eleven months older than Deena and a whole lot bigger.

The letters came pretty regular at first. They all said how much she missed us and how she couldn't wait to get home to see her girls. That's what she always called us, her "girls." When she met an old friend up on the avenue, she'd say, "Nancy, these are my girls." When we ate out, she would order for us, "Two milkshakes for my girls." It made me feel good, like I belonged just as much as Deena.

Now, I go through the mail alone. I always turn every page of the catalogs and the supermarket circulars because you never know where a thin letter could get stuck. I don't blame Deena for being mad. It's not fair that she got left behind.

"I won't help clean up unless you tell me what you found." Deena crossed her arms and glared at me.

"I can't, Deena! I'll show you later, I promise."

A couple of people wandered over to the bus stop to wait for the 8:22.

"Good morning, girls," Mrs. Fitz called.

"Good morning, Mrs. Fitz."

"What are you girls doing up and out so early?" Mrs. Fitz works in the cafeteria at Jefferson Hospital. Some days she brings us leftover soft pretzels or bagels. And since Mom left, we get other stuff from Mrs. Fitz, too, like candy bars and change that she says she found on the floor under the tables.

"It's too hot to sleep, Mrs. Fitz," I said.

George P. was nodding his head and grinning. He lives in the group home over on Tulip Street and bags groceries at the Acme.

"You're lucky, George P.," I said. "You get to be in the air-conditioned store all day."

George P. put his fist in his mouth, but he was smiling. I had started to gather up the trash and make a small pile. A man with long hair was leaning up against the wall. I had seen him around before, but I didn't know him.

"You girls should go to the movies," Mrs. Fitz said. "You can cool off there."

"Well, we *could*," Deena complained, "if Macey would share what she found. But she's keeping it all for herself."

The long-haired man turned around and stared at me. I felt a strange chill in the pit of my stomach.

"It's money," Deena said. "Isn't it, Macey?"

I opened my mouth to say no, but nothing came out. My

eyes were still locked on his. He took a long drag from his cigarette and then, without putting it out, flicked it at me.

"Hey! What's wrong with you?!" Mrs. Fitz yelled at the man.

He calmly turned, stood over Mrs. Fitz, and blew his cigarette smoke in her face. George P. scuttled behind Mrs. Fitz and clutched her arm. The guy glared at me one more time, then he stomped off.

Mrs. Fitz stroked George P.'s arm. "Don't you worry, George P., you're okay." She turned to Deena and me. "That guy must be on something," she said, fluffing her fingers through her bluish gray curls and shaking her head. "You girls should go inside. Is your dad home?"

I didn't need to be told twice. I shut and locked the door behind us. Dad was in his work clothes, sipping coffee on the couch. "Whoa!" he said. "What's going on?"

Deena curled up on his lap. She's eleven, but she's so tiny, she could be eight or nine. I sat next to Dad, and he put his arm around me.

"Nothing," I lied. I didn't want Dad to get worried and make us stay inside all day.

"There was a weird guy at the bus stop. Mrs. Fitz told us to go inside." Deena spilled the beans. "And Macey found something and she won't show it to me."

"Mace?" Dad raised his eyebrows. "That doesn't sound like you."

I slowly reached down into my pocket and pulled it out. I held my fist closed for a second or two, then I showed it to them. Half a locket, shaped like a heart, hung on a thin gold chain.

Deena's mouth dropped open. Dad held out his hand and I placed the locket in his palm. "It's beautiful, Mace," he said.

"Look close. It says *Forever* and there are some numbers—8 and 14. Do you think ...?" I took the locket back and held it in my closed fist.

"Think what?" Dad asked.

"Nothing."

"She thinks Mom left it there." Deena rolled her eyes. "Don't you, Macey?"

"Well ... she could have." I looked down at my lap, my face hot. "Her birthday is August 14, and the numbers ..." My voice trailed off.

I felt Dad take a big gulp of air and hold it in. His arm pulled me closer. I loved the way he always smelled, like clean laundry and spicy aftershave lotion. If I could freeze time, I'd have done it right then. Because mostly, my life feels slippery, like I'm sliding around all the time, about to fall with nothing to grab onto. But at that minute, I was still and I was safe.

Dad leaned forward and set his mug on the coffee table. "Mace," he said, "it's a beautiful locket, but Mom didn't put it there. She's too far away."

"But you said you didn't know where she was," I whispered.

"Well, I don't exactly know, Mace, but she's not in Philadelphia. We know that much, don't we?"

I didn't know it. Philadelphia is a big city. There are so many people. Why couldn't she have come back without us knowing? She could be in any neighborhood, in any of the apartments or houses, waiting for the right moment to come home. She might be nervous, thinking that we're angry with her or we don't want her back.

"Deena, honey, run upstairs and get my wallet for me from my dresser."

I swear I couldn't help it. One tear rolled out of the corner of my eye before I could stop it. I quickly wiped it away, but they saw. Deena stomped up the stairs.

Dad pulled me close and I buried my face in his chest. "I'm sorry," I said, swallowing the lump in my throat.

"Don't be sorry." He wrapped his arms around me. "It's okay to cry if you want to. I know it hurts."

Crying wasn't all I was sorry about. There was so much more. If I had been the perfect child, like Deena, would Mom still be here? If she had never adopted me, never had to struggle to correct my faults, would she be sitting on the couch each morning sharing the paper with Dad? It was unbearable to think about. Maybe my guilt kept me searching for clues that she was coming back. If she were home, I would feel forgiven and I would try so much harder to be a better daughter.

"Deena's mad at me," I said.

"She's not mad at you. Being mad is just Deena's way. You know what I mean?"

I nodded against his shirt. I knew, but I still didn't like her being mad at me. Mom used to get mad, too. She'd get a flash look in her eyes like fire. But worse than the angry part was that sometimes afterward, she would get real quiet and not talk to us for days. I remember lying in bed at night and hearing Dad's voice and then silence. Then Dad would talk again and there'd be more silence. Deena would put her pillow over her head. But I stayed awake and listened. Even though the silence parts felt like little knives sticking in my chest. Dad's talking rose and fell in a good way, like the sound of small waves lapping up on the beach at night. Then one day at breakfast or at dinner, Mom would cry and that meant that everything would be back to normal again.

Deena stomped back down the stairs. "Here." She plopped the wallet on the table and went out the front door, slamming it behind her.

Dad pulled out his handkerchief and offered it to me, but I didn't need it. I wasn't going to cry. "Don't worry about it, okay?" he said.

I worried about a lot of things even when I didn't want to. Like, what if something happened to Dad? I hated to think about it, but it popped into my head a lot, and the fear of it was camped out in the pit of my stomach. I tried to look cheerful. "Okay," I said. "I'm okay now."

"That's my girl." He gave me one more hug and handed me his cold cup of coffee. "Can you clean this up for me? I'm running late for work."

My getting upset about Mom was good for one thing. He never asked about the scary guy at the bus stop and didn't order Deena and me to stay inside all day.

I poured the coffee down the drain.

"Oh, Macey." Dad poked his head back in the house. "Don't

forget to stop by Grandma's and check on her. See if she needs any groceries."

I stifled a groan and turned on the faucet, splashing cold water on my face. I washed up the breakfast dishes and set them in the rack to dry. It was really Deena's day for the dishes, but I didn't mind. I owed her. When I went outside, she was sitting on the step, her back perfectly straight and her arms crossed. She didn't say anything to me. I tried to remember what Dad had said and not feel hurt.

Deena is my sister and my best friend, too. We almost always get along, but sometimes I wonder if she thinks about what it would be like if I wasn't around. I was part of the family first, but Deena is the real daughter and I came from somewhere else. I shouldn't think that way, but I don't know how to stop my mind from slipping around and wondering about bad things. Deena's got old photo albums and ancestors from Ireland and Dad's blue eyes and Mom's asthma. My wild, kinky hair and mottled skin and long legs don't fit in anywhere. Deena's got things to hold on to. I'm just floating and it makes me scared sometimes.

I picked up a few soda cans and a Gatorade bottle from the sidewalk and added them to the trash pile.

"I'm sorry, Deena," I said. "Don't be mad at me."

Ryan and Zach flew around the corner on their bikes and almost hit me. "Hey, Niner!" Ryan screeched his bike to a halt. "Kickball game on Ashdale Street in ten minutes. Can you guys come?"

Deena jumped up off the step. "We can come!" she answered.

"Nice hair, Niner." Zach laughed at me as he pedaled past. "I'm going to get Max and Joe. See you over there, Ryan."

I quickly ran my hands through my hair, smoothing it back, but I could feel the curls spring right back up. I had forgotten to brush my hair this morning, but it wouldn't have made a difference anyway.

"I gotta get changed. Wait for me, Macey." Deena darted into the house.

Ryan parked his bike. "Hey, your dad fixed up the wall."

"He did?" I hadn't even noticed. "Oh, yeah, I guess he did. It looks good." We had a bunch of loose stones, and Dad must have cemented them back in place. "Does my hair, like, really look that bad?" I asked.

"No, you're cool," Ryan said.

Deena popped out the front door. "Macey, do you have your key?"

"No, can you grab it for me? It should be on the hook."

Ryan jumped on his bike. "Don't be late. I'll pick you for my team." His hand brushed against mine as he pushed off from the wall.

"Let's go," Deena said. We walked up the street together, friends again.

"Dad says we have to stop at Grandma's today."

"Yeah, I know. We'll go later."

A whole summer day's worth of fun stretched out in front of us with only one chore to worry about. We hadn't even given a single thought to the weird guy at the bus stop. Looking back now, I can see that that was our first mistake.

3

The sun was right in my face or I might have noticed him sooner. I'm usually pretty good at noticing things. Maybe I was too intent on beating Zach. Deena told me later that he had been there for the whole game, moving a little closer to us with each play.

We like to play kickball on Ashdale Street because it's one-way and there isn't usually a lot of traffic. After rush hour, a bunch of the parked cars are gone, too, because their owners take them to work. Parked cars are in play and you can catch a ball after it has bounced off a hood, but it is not an out. You have to get it before it touches the car. One time Ryan climbed up on the bumper of a Chevy Cavalier and caught a ball before it hit the roof. But Mr. Satish happened to be looking out his window at the time and he got real mad and chased us all away. So we try not to climb up on the cars if we can help it.

When it was my turn at the plate, I noticed that my shoe was untied. Just as I bent down to fix it, Zach pitched the ball at me.

"STRIKE ONE!" he screamed.

"That was not a strike!" I cried. "Besides, there are no strikes in kickball."

Zach couldn't bear to lose, and our team was threatening. We were down two runs, but Ryan was on first and Joe was on second with only one out.

First base was the trunk of a silver Honda Civic. The car itself was too hot to touch, so Ryan kept his foot on the rear tire. "Knock it off, Zach," he called to his brother.

Zach spun and whipped the ball at Ryan, hitting him in the leg. Ryan was safely on base and didn't move. But Joe did. He took off and skidded into third. Third was a trash can lid with a rock in it. It moved sometimes, and Joe kicked it back into place.

"No stealing!" Zach retrieved the ball and pointed at Joe.

"We never called 'no stealing,' Zach," Joe said.

"Well, I'm calling it now!"

"Fine. But I'm not going back to second 'cause you just called it now." Joe crossed his arms. He was Zach's friend most of the time, and he was also the tallest kid in our whole class.

Zach's face was red when he turned to face me, and his mouth was all twisted. He wiped the sweat from his face with the sleeve of his T-shirt. "Easy out," he snarled. "Niner stinks."

I don't even know who first started calling me Niner. It's a nickname I've had with the kids at school for as long as I can remember. And I don't really mind it anymore except when it comes from Zach. He makes it sound like an insult or a curse word.

Zach rolled the ball toward me. Even though it was a perfect roll, I let it go. I know it was mean, but I couldn't help myself. I don't stink. I'm bad at a whole lot of things, but I am good at any sport that doesn't require ten fingers.

I put my hand in my pocket and ran my fingers over the chain and locket. Even if Deena and Dad did not believe it, it was a sign. It felt like a good-luck charm, like Mom was thinking of me this very minute. Something good was going to happen. I got set behind the plate.

Zach glared at me and spit one of those big, throat-clearing gobs my way. "Here you go, baby." He pitched a slow, bumpy roller. Joe took a lead off third. I like the bumpers. If you time it right and get your foot under the ball when it's off the ground, you can really send it. And I did. Tahirah was playing the outfield, in the middle of the street in front of the O'Briens' house. But I kicked it way over her head. She didn't even move, just threw her hands up in the air like "What can I do?" Joe was whooping as he crossed home plate, and Ryan gave me a big smile.

"Hoooome run, Macey McCallister!" Ryan gloated. "Her monster kick puts her team up one run!" Ryan wants to be an announcer for ESPN when he grows up.

Zach was cursing at Tahirah, as if it was all her fault, when suddenly his voice dropped. "You're out, Niner," he said quietly. "You're out."

I slowed between second and third.

"Run, Niner. Run!" Joe screamed. "Don't listen to him!"

I coasted into home and stood on the plate, which was the

bottom of an old cardboard box. Everyone else seemed frozen, staring out toward center field.

I squinted and put my hands up over my eyes.

The fattest kid I had ever seen was standing in the middle of the street with the ball tucked under his arm. If he had been any fatter, he would have blotted out the sun.

"Hey! That's our ball!" Deena yelled. "Give it back."

The kid took a few steps forward but held the ball.

Deena marched up to him, snatched the ball out of his arms, and came back to home plate. "I'm up," she said.

Zach grabbed the ball from Deena and threw it in my face. "Niner's out." Then he tapped the ball on Ryan's and Joe's shoulders. "Ryan's out and Joe's out because they're off their bases. We're up."

"No way!" Deena cried. "Macey had a home run."

"The ball was caught by that fat kid. She's out."

"She is not! That fat kid is not even in the game and you *know* that was a home run."

My eyes darted to the new kid. His expression never changed, but his shoulders seemed to melt a little.

"Deena ...," I began.

"Stay out of this, Macey!" Deena's anger was on a roll, so I kept my mouth shut.

Sometimes at school kids laugh at me when I'm fumbling with the scissors or trying to open a container. I don't mind that so much. But it's really awful when they get caught and my teacher wants to discuss the whole thing at morning meeting. Sitting in a circle, my hands hidden in my lap, I stare at the floor while they make their forced apologies and my teacher talks about how my difference makes me special. She's only trying to be nice, but she makes me feel like a specimen in the science lab. Deena and Zach were talking about this fat kid just like they would about the overfed mouse in our classroom. I knew exactly how he was feeling, and my insides cringed.

"Ty couldn't have caught that ball. It's no different than if it got stuck in a tree." Deena's hands were on her hips. She would never back down.

"She so too could've caught it!" Zach argued. "She didn't even run for it because that fat kid was back there and he was blocking her."

"Zach, I think I …," Tahirah began.

"Shut up, Ty. Give it to me, Deena." Zach lunged for the ball in Deena's hands.

"No! You're not up. We are!" Deena and Zach struggled over the ball.

Zach kicked her in the knee and she got him back in the shin, but neither one let go.

"Yo, knock it off," Ryan said.

"C'mon, you guys," Tahirah pleaded. "Let's just have a do-over or whatever."

I knew something was wrong when Deena gave up the ball. She didn't even complain that Zach was dancing around with it over his head. She looked at me and took a few steps in my direction. Then she sank to the ground.

"Deena!" I dropped down beside her. She had no air left

for fighting. She was taking short, panting breaths and her eyes were wide.

"Can't breathe," she squeaked.

"Oh, God! She's having one of her asthma attacks," Tahirah said.

Ryan grabbed home plate and started to fan Deena.

"Ryan, stop!" All he was doing was kicking up the dirt from the street. "Deena, where's your inhaler?"

"Home." Tears began to trickle out of the corners of her eyes.

"Upstairs or down?" I asked.

She shrugged.

"Stay calm, stay calm," I said. "I'll be right back."

I took off and flew down the street. My mind was racing along with my legs. Where did she last use her inhaler? She always left it lying around. I darted across Crispin Street and a gold car slammed on its brakes and blew its horn at me. I kept going. I took a shortcut up Delaney Street's back alley, running past little kids riding their Big Wheels and toddlers splashing in their plastic pools. I fumbled in my pocket for the key.

"You okay, Macey?" called Mrs. Chen, taking her laundry off the clothesline.

I waved and kept going. I slid the key into the back-door lock and rushed through the basement and upstairs. I opened the kitchen cabinet and swept the medicine bottles into my hand. No inhaler. The dining-room table was full of mail and papers, nothing more. I kept thinking about Deena gasping for air and my own throat started to hurt. If I didn't hurry, she could end up in the hospital with a mask on her face.

I checked the living-room couch, the TV stand. I ran to the front room where Deena sits by the window and reads. There it was! I saw it on her pile of books, next to a bunch of candy wrappers. I darted to pick it up. Just as I reached for it, he popped out at me.

I screamed and fell backward onto the floor.

"Open the door," he growled, his face a few feet from mine on the other side of the front picture window. "Open it now." It was the man from the bus stop. His voice was low and angry and he fixed me again with those scary eyes. I felt like I couldn't look away. I was frozen in place.

"All right, kid," he snarled. "That does it. You're going to be sorry."

For a second I knew what asthma felt like. I couldn't breathe at all.

Then his face disappeared and I saw the top of his head as he moved across the patio. I heard him climb the five steps to the front door. He shook the handle hard. I thanked God that Deena hadn't forgotten to lock up this morning. It wouldn't be long, though, before he thought of the back door and it was wide open. I grabbed the inhaler and raced into the basement, three steps at a time. I slammed the door shut. "C'mon, c'mon," I pleaded with myself. My hands were shaking so hard I had trouble fitting the key into the lock. Footsteps were coming fast from around the corner of the house. The bolt finally clicked and I sprinted up the driveway.

"Macey! Macey! You sure nothing wrong?" Mrs. Chen called after me.

I didn't even pause to wave this time. When I got to the end of the street, I ducked behind a hedge. My chest hurt from the wild pounding of my heart. I dropped to my knees on the hot cement sidewalk and carefully peeked back up toward my house. He was standing at the other end of the block, staring in my direction, smoking a cigarette.

Maybe I should have told Mrs. Chen. She's sweet and always looking out for me and Deena. She would have taken me in. I could have called the police or phoned Dad at work. But I didn't have time to sit around and figure out what to do. I was worried about Deena.

Now I can see that this was my second big mistake.

4

"Hurry up!" Ty was waiting for me at the end of Ashdale Street. She was jumping up and down, acting all panicky. "What took you so long?"

I didn't have time to say. I raced past her. Deena was sitting on the O'Briens' lawn, under a tree, and she was gasping and crying at the same time. I shook the inhaler for her and she squirted the mist into her mouth. We were all quiet while she held her breath, trying to hold the medicine in her lungs for as long as possible.

My hands were shaking. I sat on them and took some deep breaths myself. One more puff and I could see that Deena was starting to relax, even though she was still crying. I lay down next to her in the grass. I wanted so bad to tell her what had happened at our house. The feeling of it was still so sharp inside me that it hurt. But I couldn't say anything. Deena wasn't allowed to take her inhaler now for another four hours and I had to keep her calm.

The doctor always told Deena that she made things worse by getting upset. "You need to keep yourself calm," he insisted. One time Deena grabbed the little plastic pillow from the examining table and thrust it toward the doctor. "Okay. How about we stuff this pillow down your throat and see how calm you can stay?" It's true. She really said that. She had to go straight to her room when we got home and she wasn't allowed to watch television for a whole week.

But Deena says that that's what asthma feels like, a big fluffy pillow in your throat that keeps growing until you can't get any air. I wouldn't be able to stay calm either.

"What do you think that cloud looks like?" I asked, pointing at a particularly large one floating over the houses across the street. It helped a lot if she thought about something else besides the way she was breathing.

"A clown," Ty answered.

"A clown!" Deena couldn't help it. She started to laugh right in the middle of her cry. She rolled onto her side and held her stomach, half-coughing, half-giggling.

"Yeah, it's a clown. Look. See the fuzzy hair on the side and that big part that sticks out? That's the nose." Ty has a thing about clowns. She's obsessed with them. It's very strange.

"It's a horse's head," Deena insisted.

All I could see was that scary guy's face and his mean gray eyes staring at me through the window. His face was in the cloud and in the tree and just about anywhere I looked. I kept glancing up and down the street, worried that he might have followed me.

Ryan came screeching up on his bike. "You okay now, Deena?"

"Yeah. Ryan, what do you see in that cloud?" Deena sat up.

Ryan twisted around on his bike and looked up in the sky

for a moment. "I don't know. Looks like a big cotton ball or something."

Ty was doing cartwheels on the sidewalk. "What? A cotton ball! Ry, you have no imagination."

"Well, I just came back to let you guys know that we can't finish the game. Me and Zach have baseball practice this afternoon."

"Yeah, well, you tell Zach that we WON the kickball game." Deena started to cough hard. "Macey won it with her home-run kick."

"Yeah, okay. I'll be sure to tell him that. Whoa, Macey, you don't look too good either."

Deena seemed to see me for the first time. "What's the matter? You are kind of pale."

"Nothing. It's just the heat. I'm fine."

Ryan pedaled off. Most of the kids had already wandered away. I got behind Deena and pounded my hands up and down her back. Sometimes that helped her with the coughing fits. One time when I was working on Deena like this and she was crying hard, Mom came running into the room and pulled me backward by the collar of my shirt and hit me across the face. "What are you doing?" she screamed. "Don't you ever hit my baby!" I started to cry, too. In the next second, she saw the inhaler in Deena's hand and knew what was happening. She felt bad and suddenly I was her girl again, and she treated me special all day. It was the only time she ever hit me.

"It's a mountain, with snow on the top, and if you look close you can see a little village at the bottom."

I stopped pounding on Deena and looked for the person who spoke. It was the fat kid. Believe it or not, I hadn't noticed him. He was sitting above us, in the shadow of the O'Briens' house.

"What are you talking about?" Deena asked.

"The cloud," he said. "Look."

"That's almost as stupid as the cotton ball." Deena laughed.

But I could see it. The village was nice and peaceful and I started to wish that I could go there. It would be cool and no one would flick cigarettes at you or try to break into your house. Deena, Ty, and the fat kid were arguing about the cloud.

"What do you think, Macey?" Ty asked.

I shrugged. "Don't ask me." My problem was I could see it all three ways. The peak of the mountain turned into the clown's hat turned into the ear of the horse poking up out of its soft mane. I could see everybody else's idea, but I could never find one of my own. I liked the mountain one the best, though.

"Macey, you ain't got no imagination either," Ty scolded.

"Yeah, that's why she likes Ryan," Deena said. "No imagination."

"Deena!" I shoved her in the shoulder. "Shut up. I do not."

I saw the fat kid looking at me and felt my face start to burn. "Hey, what's your name?" I asked. I had to find out soon before I slipped and called him "fat kid" to his face.

"Eugene."

"Huge-een?" Deena was being smart and I poked her.

"I'm Macey, that's Deena, and that's Tahirah, but we call her Ty for short."

"Those are weird names," Eugene said.

"Oh yeah, HUGE-een?" Deena spat. "Well I think HUGE-een is a weird name, even though it is kind of perfect for you."

"I like it," Eugene answered. "It was my dad's name and my grandfather's name, so it's kind of a tradition in our house."

"Kind of like being rude is a tradition in his house," Deena said to me.

It was wicked hot out that day. The grass was brown and prickly and the leaves on the tree above us were drooping. There wasn't a breath of air anywhere. Deena started coughing again, trying to get rid of whatever was stuck in her lungs. Much as I hated it, we had to go to our grandmother's house. She had an air-conditioner in her front window, and Deena needed that cool air. Also, I wanted her away from Eugene before she got into a fight and got herself all worked up again.

"We gotta go," I announced.

"Why? Where you goin'?" Ty asked.

"We have to go to our grandmother's."

"You can come, Ty," Deena teased.

"Nooooo way. I ain't that desperate for something to do."

"I'll come," Eugene said.

For a moment nobody spoke. I should have said something right away, but I was trying to think of the best way to explain things.

"Believe me, you don't want to go," Ty finally told him.

Eugene shrugged. "I got nothing else to do."

"Yeah, well, you'd be better off sitting here watching the

grass wither," Ty said. "You'd have more fun gettin' stung by a swarm of bees or bein' attacked by a pack o' wild dogs or—"

"Okay, Huge-een, you can come," Deena announced. "Why not?" She winked at me.

I knew why not. I should have said something, but I didn't. This is the problem with being a slow thinker. Everything is all decided before you even figure out what you want to say.

Ty laughed and made a fake sign of the cross over us as we got up to leave. I didn't think the situation was very funny, though. I felt tired as I trudged up the street after Deena and Eugene. Besides the fact that we were headed for a disaster at Grandma's, now I couldn't talk to Deena alone about what had happened at our house. So I just followed along. I didn't say anything. I didn't do anything. That was another mistake. They were piling up faster now than snowflakes in a blizzard.

5

"How come you have only nine fingers?" Eugene asked.

We were standing at the corner on Tabor Road. The cars were zipping past, whipping dust up in our faces, which was definitely not good for Deena's breathing. I stood in front of her and pushed the button for the green light even though it didn't ever work. We timed it one day when we were bored, Ty and Deena and Ryan and me. We took turns either pushing the button or not pushing it, and seeing if there was any difference in how long it took the light to change. We proved that the button was useless. I wanted to use our experiment as my science project, but Deena said that was stupid.

I pushed the button anyway just because it was there. That's when Eugene noticed my missing thumb. I slid my hand in my pocket.

Deena jumped in front of him and thrust her finger in his face. "How come you're so fat, HUGE-een?" she asked.

"It's a glandular problem." He didn't seem to mind the question. "I'm going to a summer program at Children's Hospital for kids who have the same condition. That's why I'm here. I'm staying with my aunt."

"Oh." Deena dropped her hand to her side. She seemed to look at Eugene in a new way. "Are all the kids there as overweight as you?"

Deena probably thought she was being nice by saying "overweight" instead of "fat." The light turned green and we started across the street. Nice or not, Deena's question was stupid. The fat from Eugene's legs spilled over his ankles and rested on his sneaker tops and sweat was leaking out of the folds of skin on his neck. His shirt was completely drenched. Eugene could be in the *Guinness Book of World Records* for childhood fatness and no kid in the world could even come close to him.

Eugene shrugged. "I don't know. I didn't see everybody yet."

"Well, is *any*body there fatter than you?" she pressed.

Dad says that Deena's mouth works at the same speed as her brain and sometimes she needs to slow down. This was one of those times. I have the opposite problem. My brain works real slow and my mouth works even slower. Mom used to get frustrated when she tried to help me with my homework, especially the math. Hard as I try, I just cannot make sense of number problems or formulas, and it didn't matter if Mom drew pictures or explained it ten different ways, it still looked like Chinese to me. Also, I cannot see the point in any of it. Why would a person learn Chinese if they are never going to China? I am never going to be a mathematician like Mom. Before Deena was born, Mom used to teach calculus in a private high school, and in the summers she gave seminars to business people. She still has all her files neatly organized and color-coded in a cabinet in case she needs them again. A place for everything and everything in its place, she always said. I can't even organize the clothes in my closet.

One night when Mom was trying to teach me how to find areas and circumferences and other such stuff, I told her my theory about Chinese and math. She got upset. "I am going out for some air," she said. My aunt Kate was visiting that night. She told me that Mom was a math whiz when she was in school. She won all the school prizes and placed in the state math competitions. Aunt Kate patted me on the arm. "But don't worry. It's not your fault that you can't do math," she said. "It's not as if you could take after her, right?"

That was true. I couldn't take after Mom. I didn't have any of her genes. She thought she could pour all her math knowledge into my head, but it didn't work. It all flowed in one ear and right out the other without ever touching my brain. My math skills are like my thumb. They're just not there. Dad said once that he was never good at math either. So sometimes I pretend that I take after him. I am happy, though, that Deena is smart and gets all A's in math. It made Mom proud. And besides, Mom did cheer for me at soccer games. I remember that.

"Seven, maybe eight," he said, counting off on his fingers as he walked, "are fatter than me. But I knew some kids at home who were bigger."

"Wow." Deena let out a long breath and I heard the whistle in her lungs.

"One kid named Todd was so fat," Eugene continued, "that

he couldn't even walk. He had an electric wheelchair and he decorated it with racing-car stripes. One time I heard he got stuck in the doorway of his doctor's office and they couldn't get him out for, like, three or four days."

"No way. What did they do?"

"Well, they didn't give him anything to eat for those three or four days and he lost enough weight so that he finally squeezed through. And the very next day the doctor put in a wider door so that no one would ever get stuck again."

I wondered if that boy's mother or father stayed with him all that time. And what did they do when he had to go to the bathroom? It was an ugly picture. I shuddered at the thought. Or maybe I shuddered because we had arrived at Grandma's house.

"Eugene," I said. "You better wait outside."

I saw him look longingly at the air-conditioner humming in the front window of the row house.

"I won't get stuck in the door," he said. "I promise."

"Eugene, I didn't mean—"

"And I'll sit on the floor, too, 'cause I'm all sweaty. I can't really help it. It's my glands."

"C'mon, Eugene. Don't worry about it." Deena unlocked the door and waved him inside.

A wall of cool air washed over me and I shivered. It smelled like old couch cushions and stale baby powder and last night's dinner. It smelled like, well …, like Grandma.

Grandma was asleep in her chair by the front picture window, her mouth open, her glasses sitting all the way down at the end of her nose. We tiptoed into the cramped kitchen. The little table fit only two chairs, so Eugene sat on the floor back by the cellar door. Deena made lemonade. Grandma doesn't like me to touch her things, or I would have offered to help. I broke her pitcher once a while back, so I don't blame her for not trusting me. Having nine fingers makes me clumsier than most.

"Macey, get me the ice," Deena whispered.

"But—"

"She's *asleep!*" Deena hissed.

Grandma doesn't like me to open the fridge either. I'm not sure about the reason for that one. I slid out the ice cube trays and set them on the counter.

Deena carefully pulled three glasses from the cabinet.

"Can I have a clean one?" I asked.

She looked in the bottoms of all three. "There aren't any clean ones."

I wished I wasn't so thirsty.

"Don't worry," Deena said, turning toward Eugene. "It's nothing that'll kill you."

Grandma wasn't too good at washing up anymore. Her plates had little pieces of food stuck to them, and most of her glasses had dried-up milk rings in the bottom. It gave my stomach a funny feeling to drink lemonade and see that crusty white line in it. I closed my eyes and pretended it wasn't there. That's why I didn't see Eugene get up. He can be pretty quiet for such a big kid.

"Where's he goin'?" I asked Deena.

"He had to go to the bathroom."

"Oh, great." The only bathroom in the house was upstairs. Eugene would have to sneak through the living room to get there.

"Stop worrying about everything." Deena poured herself a second glass. The air conditioning was helping her. The color was coming back into her face and she hadn't coughed once since we got into the house.

I peeked into the living room. Grandma was still asleep. Eugene must have safely made it up the steps. Deena sat across from me at the little table.

"Are you feeling better?"

"Yeah. I'm fine. Will you stop fussing? You're worse than Mom." Deena's eyes flashed for a minute. She tried to get up from the table, but I grabbed her arm. She'd think it was my fault that she said "Mom," and now she'd be mad at me.

"No," I said. "I was asking because ... well, never mind. Deena, remember that guy at the bus stop?"

"Yeah, so what?" She pulled her arm away from me.

"When I went home to get your inhaler, he was there, outside the window. He tried to get in our house."

"What?!"

"He told me to let him in. I wouldn't, of course. What if he tried to hurt me? But then he started pulling on the door."

"What did you do?!" Deena was breathing fast, but I didn't hear any wheezes.

"I ran out the back door. Mrs. Chen was there. I think she saw him."

"Did you tell her what he did?"

"No, I—"

A scream came from the other room and I knew it didn't come from Grandma. Deena and I jumped up and ran into the living room.

"Call the police!" Grandma cried. "Call the police! 9-1-1!"

Eugene was crouched at the bottom of the stairs and Grandma was hitting him in the head with a flyswatter.

"Grandma!" Deena yelled. "Stop that. He's our friend. This is Eugene. Eugene, this is our grandma." Deena finally pronounced his name the right way.

"Hello," Eugene croaked.

"Well!" was all that Grandma said. She uses a walker to get around, but she's quicker than you would think. She turned and marched back to her chair. "Deena, come here, girl."

Eugene slumped to the floor and I sat above him on the second step.

"Who is that boy?" she demanded.

"I told you, Grandma, he's our friend."

"He's fat."

"Grandma!"

"Well, he is! It don't make any sense to pretend. But I'll keep it to myself."

Eugene's shoulders melted a little again. I'm not sure why Grandma thinks that other people can't hear the things she says about them. One time when I was little, Deena and I were playing with a puzzle on the floor and the grown-ups were sitting around talking. It got quiet for a minute and then

Grandma looked down at me and said, "I'll never know why you had to get a colored one."

Grandma and Mom started shouting. Dad picked me up and walked right out the front door. It was cold and we had left our coats behind. But I didn't care. He held me real tight and carried me all the way home.

I didn't know what all the fuss was about. I thought Grandma had been talking about the puzzle. But when Deena came home she said that they were fighting about me. We both looked at me in the mirror on our bureau. We looked a long time trying to find the colors, but we didn't see any. So we played with the nail polish. I painted Deena's freckles red and blue and she put green stars on my cheeks.

When Mom came in to say good night, she cried when she saw us and we felt bad. Dad washed our faces and tucked us in. He hugged me extra long before he turned out the lights. Mom didn't talk to him for a whole week, but she treated me special. I felt like something was my fault, but I didn't know what. We didn't visit Grandma for a long time after that.

"Don't listen to her." I leaned down and whispered to Eugene. "She's kind of senile, you know."

But Eugene didn't say anything. It takes a little while to get used to Grandma. No law says that you have to like everyone in the world. Grandma doesn't have to like me. I'd get annoyed, too, if somebody I didn't like, for example, Zach, stopped over my house a lot and spent all his holidays with me. I try to think of it like that and then it makes sense, sort of.

"Grandma," Deena said. "We're going to the store for you. Do you have a list?"

"I saw him go up the steps, you know, how could I miss it? But I pretended to be asleep. Oh, my heart! I didn't know you girls were in the kitchen. I got my flyswatter. It was sitting right here because somebody let a fly in yesterday. Look, there it goes." Grandma took a swipe at the fly and it buzzed into the other room. "I saw him start up the steps. I pretended to be asleep, but—"

"Grandma, we *know*," Deena moaned. "Do you have a list for the store?"

She dabbed her handkerchief under each eye. "Oh, my heart," she repeated. "You don't know how scared I was."

She wasn't really crying, but she was rocking in her chair so hard that the back of it kept banging against the wall.

Deena crossed her arms real tight. "Grandma, please stop it. It was just our friend and you know it now, so where's the list?"

Grandma sniffed a few times and wiped at her nose. "Just wait till you're old. See how you feel when nobody cares about *your* feelings."

I got up from the step and knelt beside her chair. I put my hand on her arm and she was actually shaking. "We're sorry, Grandma. You must have been real scared."

"I was. I was." She curled away from me. I had touched her with the wrong hand.

"I'd be scared, too, if I saw a stranger in the house." I could sympathize because I was terrified when that man popped his face up at our window. "But Eugene's not a stranger. He's our friend. Do you want me to get you something to drink?"

"I pretended I was asleep. Then I got my flyswatter."

"GRANDMA!" Deena stomped her foot on the floor. "You told us that three times already."

I went to look for the list. It wasn't on the fridge, the counter, or the windowsill. I finally found it on the dining-room table under the bowl with the dusty plastic fruit. I folded it and put it in my back pocket.

"Okay," I said. "I got it. Let's go."

"She wants to see your necklace." Deena stared at me with pursed lips.

"What?" My hand darted to my pocket. "But how—"

"I had to change the subject somehow." Deena shrugged.

"No."

But Grandma was already out of her chair, cornering me with her walker. I backed up against the fake brick fireplace, knocking my head on the mantel.

"Let's see," Grandma demanded. "Give it to me."

I wouldn't have shown her, but she was right in my face and I was trapped. Eugene looked away.

Now I was the one who was shaking. I slowly pulled out the locket. I held it in my ugly hand so that she wouldn't touch it. But she did. She pulled it away from me and held it up in front of her smudged glasses.

"Do you remember our mom ever having a locket like that?" Deena asked. "Macey thinks her birth date is on it and it's hers."

I felt like Deena had hit me. She was on the other side of the room, but I felt it.

"Your mother," Grandma spat. "She was no good from the start. I told him—how many times did I tell him?—not to marry her. Thought she was so much better than us with her fancy school degrees." She lowered her voice but only from a yell to a shout. "*She's* the one who wanted *her*." Grandma's index finger was in my face, almost touching my nose. "And then she runs off and leaves your father holdin' the bag. I told him. ..."

I don't remember how I got away from her, but I stumbled out the door and into the heat. My chest hurt, like somebody was standing on it. I dropped onto the bottom step and held my head in my hands. Eugene appeared beside me. He didn't say anything. He just sat there and looked at the ground. I was real embarrassed.

Grandma says a lot of things and I know better than to believe her. But what if Mom had wanted to adopt a baby and Dad didn't? Dad would give in, because he always does. He had told me the story so many times about how I stole his heart in the very first moment that we met. But maybe he didn't really want me before then. Maybe Dad and Mom and Deena would still be together, a whole family, if I had never come along. The thought of Dad not wanting me, even for a second, made the pain in my chest almost unbearable.

And then a weird thing happened. Eugene put his big, heavy arm across my shoulder. He was sweaty and smelly, but I didn't flinch because he was trying to be nice and it feels bad when people flinch away from you. Besides, it wasn't so awful anyway.

Deena finally came outside.

"Look, Macey. It's not Mom's, and Grandma says so, too." She said it kind of soft, like she felt bad. But I didn't answer her. I put my hand over my empty pocket and I wished that I had never shown the necklace to Deena.

"It's just some stupid broken necklace." Her voice rose with every word. "And now you know the truth. It's better than you carrying it around and pretending that she's coming back all the time." She kicked the step, and some loose cement crumbled to the sidewalk. "I don't want her to come back anyway. We don't need her. So just *stop*."

She didn't really mean it, but I couldn't look at her and I couldn't say anything. A fist-sized lump was stuck in my throat.

Deena turned away from me. "C'mon, Eugene. Do you want to come to the store and help carry? Macey's going to mope."

She was right again. I did mope. I dragged myself behind them. I wanted my necklace back. I wanted Mom back. If I was like Deena, I could have gotten control of myself and been strong. Maybe my birth mother moped a lot and that's who I take after.

Deena marched liked a soldier straight ahead, arms swinging, but Eugene turned around once in a while to steal a peek at me. In a weird way, it made me feel less miserable.

6

"I love hot dogs," Eugene said, plopping down in a kitchen chair. "They are my favorite food."

I was kind of wondering whether Eugene really had a glandular problem. He bought two Snickers bars and a Coke at the grocery store and finished them before we even got back to Grandma's house. To be fair, he did buy one of the candy bars for me, but I didn't want it.

Eugene followed us home and I asked him to stay for dinner. Deena shot me a look, but since she's not talking to me, I wasn't sure if she was mad about the invitation or about something else. She shouldn't have cared because it was my night to make dinner. We were having hot dogs and baked beans.

I was slicing the hot dogs and mixing them in the pot with the baked beans when Ty appeared at the kitchen door. Deena was reading one of her books in the living room.

"Hey, Macey."

I unlatched the screen door. "Come on in, Ty. You want to stay for dinner?" I turned the burner on low.

Ty looked down into the pot and rolled her eyes. "Macey,

didn't your mother teach you anything?" Ty wasn't afraid to talk about Mom like some other kids.

"Yeah," I said. "She taught me to cut up the hot dogs real small before I threw them in the pot."

"You lie." Ty laughed. "If your mother knew that you were cookin' that stuff, she'd come back and beat you."

It's true that Mom was a wonderful cook. She made special dinners for holidays and birthdays and sometimes for no reason at all. She taught me how to iron the tablecloth and set the plates with the knife on the right, the blade facing in, and the forks on the left. She always arranged a spray of flowers in the center and folded the napkins in a kind of fan shape. It was cool. The flowers, napkins, tablecloth, and even the candles were always perfectly color-coordinated. We had soup spoons for the soup and salad forks for the salad. There were salt and pepper shakers for every season and she always kept them filled to the top. Everything had to be perfect for our special dinners. One time I spilled the cranberries when I was putting them on the table and it spoiled everything. She didn't get mad at me, but I caught her crying in the kitchen. And she hardly ate any dinner at all, just sat there staring at the big red blotch right in the middle of her beautiful table. That night she and Dad lingered for hours in the dining room with a candle between them, drinking wine. I curled up on the couch with the TV on and watched them on the sly. Later, when Mom went out for a long walk, I helped Dad clean up. He sang silly songs to make me laugh while I dried the dishes. We tried to clean the tablecloth, but the stain wouldn't come out. "It's just a stupid tablecloth," Deena had said.

I'm not real picky when it comes to food and neither is Deena. So we don't mind that the dinners aren't fancy anymore. What we miss are the times we would bake together. Mom made the best apple pies in the whole world. I always got to sprinkle the sugar over the apples, and Deena squirted them with a lemon. I asked one time why I always did the sugar and Mom said, "Because you're so sweet." After that, I didn't care that I didn't get a turn with the lemon. When she was done squeezing, Deena and I would put the lemon in our mouths and laugh at the funny faces we made.

"I love hot dogs," Eugene said again.

"Yeah, he likes hot dogs, Ty."

"Well, maybe you two ought to get married, then. What's Deena doin'?"

"Reading." I pointed with my spoon to the living room.

"I'll put a stop to that." Ty laughed and headed for the other room.

Our house is pretty small. Even though Deena was on the couch, she was only about ten steps away from where I stood cooking at the range. I watched because Ty's really funny. When she couldn't distract Deena with talking, she started to dance. Ty's built like the scarecrow in *The Wizard of Oz*, all loose and double-jointed. She was cracking me up, and even Deena was beginning to smile. I had just motioned for Eugene to get up and take a look when I saw something. A fire flashed in my chest and I couldn't breathe.

It passed in front of the living-room window. I was sure I saw the top of someone's head!

"Eugene! Lock that kitchen door!" I yelled and sprinted to the living room. I threw my body up against the door, slammed it shut, and turned the lock in one quick motion.

Ty was frozen in mid-dance. "Mace? Are you out of your mind or something?"

I stared at Deena. "Someone was on the patio," I panted. "Just now. Did you see him?"

"Yeah, I saw him." Deena yawned.

"Me, too. I think he liked my dancin'," Ty said. "But how come you're afraid of the mailman all of a sudden?"

I stared down at my feet. Bills and junky circulars were scattered all around me. I sunk to the floor. It was just the mailman. "It's kind of late for the mail, don't you think?" I squeaked.

"Yeah, it is," Deena said. "I don't think it was the regular guy."

"Maybe the regular guy got bit by a dog or something," Ty offered. "Dogs hate mailmen."

"They're called postal carriers," Deena corrected.

"Yeah, them, too," Ty said. "Macey, what are you all freaked out about?"

"I thought it was him."

"Who?" Ty sat across from me on the floor.

"This guy who was at the bus stop this morning. He was weird, in a mean kind of way."

"What'd he do?" Eugene moved closer and leaned up against the front window.

"I don't know. Nothing, really. He scared me when he looked at me. He was angry, like I did something to him."

"He flicked a cigarette at you," Deena added.

"Yeah, he did that. And Mrs. Fitz was there and he blew smoke in her face. George P. got scared."

"He scared George P.? Man, that's really low. I would have told him off, that's what I would've done."

"Yeah, but the worst part is that he came back. When Deena had her asthma attack and I ran back to get her inhaler, he was here. He tried to get into the house."

"What?!" Ty rolled backward on the floor and did a complete reverse tumble. "You got to call the police, Macey. That's like some kind of crime, trying to get into a person's house. It's illegal entering or something or other. It was on TV one time."

I looked over at Deena. She was biting her thumbnail. We were thinking the same thing.

"I'm going to talk to my dad about it tonight," I said.

"Yeah, but don't you say anything to anybody, Ty," Deena warned. "We'll take care of it. And you neither, Eugene."

Eugene shrugged. "Okay. Your dad'll probably—"

"You're not going to talk to your dad at all, are you?" Ty crossed her arms and shook her head at us.

We weren't. We had good reasons. In the beginning, after Mom went on her trip, Deena and I had to stay inside all the time when Dad was at work. He's a mechanic in the maintenance yard at SEPTA and he fixes the buses and trolleys that break down. He worried constantly and called us whenever he could, but lots of times he couldn't get to the phone until his break. He asked Mrs. Chen to check in on us every day.

She's a nice lady with three little girls who are real sweet and cute. She cares about us, but she can be hard to understand, especially on the phone. She's still working on her English skills. One time when she called to ask if we were okay, Deena was in a bad mood and she told her that we were fine, fine, fine. But Mrs. Chen thought we had a fire, fire, fire. It's a long story, but it ended up with fire engines and Dad getting called out of work.

Dad's loosened up some since then, and we want it to stay that way. Deena and I don't worry him about the small stuff like the kids who broke the window up at Mick's last week. And we shrugged our shoulders when Dad asked us how the paperboy got such a black eye even though we knew that he had gotten robbed when he was making his rounds. Bad stuff happens sometimes and we can't go living our whole lives cooped up in the house. After all, I am twelve and I can take care of myself.

"You should tell your dad," Eugene said. "Even if you don't tell the police, you should tell your dad."

Deena whipped around on him. "That's *our* decision," she snapped.

"I didn't say it wasn't." Eugene looked out the window and fiddled with the cord for the blinds. "But I would tell my dad if it was me."

"Well, good for you. Come here. Everybody put their hand in."

Ty groaned. "Not another swearing thing. I ain't letting you poke me with no pin again."

"No, we won't do the blood swear. Just a plain one."

We hunched close in a circle and put our hands together. Deena made us repeat three times that we wouldn't tell anyone about what happened on pain of death. Sometimes she gets a little overdramatic. Eugene went along with it, but he kept shaking his head and he never took his eyes off mine during the swear. It was like he was trying to tell me something. Deena said later she thought that Eugene went along because he needed friends and didn't want us to get mad. I think now that that had nothing to do with it. Eugene had some secrets of his own that he wasn't sharing and he knew all too well how to keep his mouth shut.

We were all stupid. Even though we were supposed to be serious and we were swearing about something dangerous and scary, I felt happy. We had four hands stacked together, one tiny and white, one bigger and black, one fat and damp, and one missing a thumb, but nobody seemed to mind. It was like—I don't know—like we were all normal.

I always concentrate on the wrong things—our hands instead of our words. Eugene ended up being right even though we never really listened to him or gave him a chance to talk. And if that wasn't bad enough, we held to our swear even after what happened later that night.

7

I could tell that something was up the minute Dad walked in the door.

"Hey, Dad." Deena gave him a wave. "Macey invited a friend for dinner. Is that okay?"

"Sure," he answered, flipping his keys onto the end table and smiling at Eugene.

I put my arms around his chest and hugged him. Deena sighed. She thinks I am too old to be running up and hugging him every day when he gets home. I don't know how to explain it to her, how it makes me feel when he comes in the door. Deena doesn't see how shaky the world is and how everything is always changing. I used to think that was because she was almost a whole year younger than me. But that wasn't it. She is so strong that she doesn't need anybody but herself. If you dropped Deena down in the middle of a desert somewhere, she would figure out what to do and she would survive. Me, I'd sink to the ground and die on the spot. Deena's got Dad's genes inside her, keeping her going, but all I've got is him. If he didn't come home from work one day, I'd have nothing left. I worry about the things that could hurt him, like speeding cars and terrorists and drug dealers with guns.

Dad's probably told me one hundred times that nothing's going to happen to him. "I'll always be here for you," he says when I worry. And he pats his chest with his hand over his heart, like it's an oath. But still, the fear of it nags me.

"What's this?" I asked, pulling a ticket from the front pocket of Dad's shirt.

"Macey, you're forgetting your manners," he said.

"Oh, sorry. Dad, this is Eugene. Eugene, this is my dad."

"Pleased to meet you, Eugene." Dad stuck out his hand, and he and Eugene shook.

I laughed. It looked funny to me, Eugene's flabby arm jiggling up and down and his whole face going red.

"Macey?" Dad raised his eyebrows at me.

"Sorry." I stared down at the ticket in my hand. "Are you going to the Phillies game?" I asked.

Deena jumped off the couch. "Can I come?" she begged.

The Phillies have a new ballpark and we have never been there. Tickets are expensive. We were planning to go once with the Boys and Girls Club outing, but I got sick the night before and Dad wouldn't go without me. Deena still reminds me of that.

Deena pulled the ticket from my hand. "Wow! This is one of those really expensive tickets, isn't it? Are they great seats?"

"Yeah, but I'm not going," Dad said. "Mr. Henley had tickets and he was giving them out to some of the guys in the garage. I told him I couldn't go, but he wouldn't take the ticket back. Told me to give it to whoever I wanted."

"I'll go!" Deena shouted.

Dad shook his head. "And how do you plan to get there?"

"Well, I could take the Frankford El to 15th Street and transfer to the Broad Street line ..."

Dad groaned.

"... but since I know you won't let me, you could take me and pick me up after it was over."

"And Macey ...," Dad began.

"And Macey wouldn't care because it was her fault that we didn't get to go last time and ..."

"You should go, Dad," I said. "We'll be fine here." Dad loves baseball. He was a big star in high school, and everybody always says that he could have made it to the major leagues if he hadn't gotten hurt.

"Yeah, Dad, why not?" Deena asked. She knew she had lost.

"Because it'll be too late and I've been gone all day and you girls would be alone."

"I'll stay with them, sir," Eugene offered.

Dad turned and took a long look at Eugene.

I almost laughed again, but I held it inside.

"We can take care of *ourselves*." Deena was mad, but she did a good job of controlling herself. Eugene wasn't much older than we were and I don't know why he thought he could protect us. Maybe because he was a boy. I knew Deena was thinking the same thing because her jaw was clenched real tight and her eyes were all squinty.

As it turned out, Eugene wasn't thinking about protecting us. He had his own reasons for wanting to stay at our house.

But we jumped to the wrong conclusion. This is why I have a hard time making decisions about anything. How can you decide when there is so much you don't know? And lots of times, you don't even know that you don't know. I'm glad now that I didn't laugh at Eugene and that Deena didn't get into a fight with him.

Dad liked being called "sir" and he acted like he was impressed with Eugene's offer. It reminded me of when Deena and I were little and Dad would go out to games with his friends. "You two take care of Mommy while I'm gone," he'd say with a wink. And after he left, Mom would ask us if we would take her up the avenue for some ice cream.

"Won't your parents want you at home, young man? The Phillies game won't end till 10:30 or so. That's pretty late to be out."

"Oh no, sir. I'm sure they won't mind. I'm staying with my aunt right now, and I'll ask her permission first, of course."

Deena was rolling her eyes big time, but Dad didn't seem to notice.

"Well, let me think about it while I get changed. I don't know if I want to go or not."

As soon as Dad went upstairs I pulled Eugene into the kitchen.

"Is it okay?" he asked, staring at his fingers. "I mean, if you and Deena don't want me to stay ..."

"It's okay," I said. "We don't mind. My dad really likes that you're gonna stay. It'll make him feel better." Dad says compliments are free and valuable so you should give them out whenever you can. What I said wasn't exactly true, but it looked like Eugene could use a boost.

"Really?"

"Yeah. I could tell. Do you want to help me set the table?"

I yelled into the living room. "Ty, do you want us to set you a place?"

She groaned. "Yeah, I guess so. But I gotta go ask my mom." She ran through the kitchen but paused at the back door. "Want me to pick up some Alka-Seltzer while I'm out?"

I threw a hot pad at her and missed. We could hear her laughing all the way down the alleyway.

Eugene's eyes met mine and we both smiled.

It was weird. I had just met Eugene today and here we were setting the table together for dinner. I felt comfortable with him. I wasn't sure why.

"You want to call home?" I asked.

He looked away from me. "Maybe in a little while."

Despite Ty's groaning, we had a great dinner. Ty's mom sent her back with two loaves of this special bread that she makes. I don't know what it's called, but it's got honey in it and I could eat the whole thing all by myself. Ty's mom is from Liberia and that's where she learned to make it.

"My mom cried into the dough when she heard you were having hot dogs for dinner, so the bread might be a little salty." Ty passed the basket of bread around the table.

"You lie," I said. "She baked that bread earlier today."

"Yeah, well, it's Thursday, right? She could just sense it."

It's true. I'm not too creative. Thursday night is hot dog

night. There could be tears in that bread. I looked at my piece kind of funny, a little worried about putting somebody's tears into my mouth.

Ty busted out laughing at me, but she had a mouthful of milk, and before she could swallow, some of it shot out of her nose.

"EEEwwww, gross!" Deena yelled.

Eugene started laughing so hard that he choked on his hot dog and ended up spitting it into his napkin.

"That does it," Deena snapped. "I've lost my appetite." And she jumped up from the table.

We held our breath until she was safely upstairs and then we exploded. Ty giggled so hysterically, she fell under the table, which got Eugene going again.

"All right, young lady," Dad said, pulling her up into her chair. "I don't want you getting hurt." But even Dad was laughing.

Ty had tears running down her face and wiped them on her sleeve. "Uh-oh," she said, looking at the empty chair across the table, "now Deena's gonna be mad at me."

I answered without thinking. "Join the club," I moaned.

Dad put his hand on my arm. "Something else happen today that I need to know about?"

"No, nothing," I lied. But my hand automatically went to my pocket and felt around for the necklace that wasn't there.

Dad patted my arm. He knew I was lying, but he didn't say anything more. He turned his attention to our guests. "Eugene," he said, "are you new to the neighborhood?"

"Yes, sir."

"Where you from?"

Eugene paused while he swallowed a hunk of bread. "Lots of places. Florida mainly."

"So this hot weather we're having doesn't bother you too much. You're probably used to it. Ketchup?" Dad passed the bottle down the table.

I don't think Eugene was too used to it because he was sweating up a storm. I slipped him a few extra napkins under the table. Perspiration was running from his hair down the sides of his head, and he had some drops on his chin that looked real close to sprinkling the food on his plate. I was glad Deena was upstairs.

I stirred the hot dog slices around on my plate, but I couldn't eat. I kept thinking about Deena showing my locket to Grandma today and Grandma saying that Dad didn't want to adopt me. I could feel Dad watching me and I wished I could somehow sneak my hot dogs to Eugene. He was already helping himself to thirds. I put a few baked beans in my mouth so that Dad wouldn't worry, but they wouldn't go down. I just kept passing them from the inside of one cheek to the other. Dad always keeps a sharp watch on what I eat even though I have been doing much better lately.

About a week after Mom left on the bus, I started having trouble eating. Dad tried to make all my favorite foods even though he's pretty hopeless as a cook. Deena used some of her allowance money and bought me a whole box of Mallo Cups, which are my favorite candy in the whole world. And I tried to eat. I really did. Aunt Kate visited and when I couldn't swallow even a bite of her special noodle casserole, she told me that I was being plain silly. "Your mother's going to be back in a week or two," she said. "So stop fussing and worrying everybody half to death."

I didn't want to worry anybody, especially Dad. I tiptoed downstairs late one night and told him I was sorry. I was going to eat again as soon as my stomach let me. He was sitting on the couch still dressed in his work clothes, watching one of those old black-and-white movies. "It's okay, Mace. It's probably my cooking," he joked. "It ruins even my big appetite." But I knew he understood because he had given up sleep in the same way that I had given up food. Looking back, I think my body knew before my head did that Mom was not coming back real soon. Since I'm on my fourth mother, I have a kind of sixth sense about being left behind. Deena says that that's stupid because those were completely different situations. But how does she know? Why did my birth mother not want me? Why did my foster mothers turn me over to someone else? I wonder what was so wrong with me even as a baby that they could hold me in their arms and decide I wasn't worth keeping. And Mom. She stayed longer, but in the end she left me, too.

Dad let me stay up that night and watch TV with him. We didn't talk much, just sat close together on the couch, his arm around my shoulder. He never told me, like Aunt Kate and Deena, that I was being silly, and he didn't reassure me that Mom would be back in no time. He knew the same as my stomach knew. I fell asleep leaning against him. When I woke up, he had already left for work and the green blanket from his bed, still smelling like both of my parents, was tucked all around me.

After dinner, Dad called me upstairs. I left Ty and Eugene in the kitchen, clearing the plates. He was in his bedroom, wearing his red Phillies T-shirt.

"You're sure everything's okay?" he asked.

"I'm sure, Dad."

He took my face in his hands and kissed my forehead. "You didn't eat much."

"I know. But sometimes I'm just not hungry. I've been eatin' fine."

"Okay," he sighed. "Let's go check on your sister, then."

But I didn't move. "Can I ask you a question first?"

"Sure. Shoot."

But now that I had opened my mouth, I was already changing my mind. It would be a mistake to ask. "It's really nothing. Never mind."

"No," Dad said. "Go ahead." He sat on the bed and motioned for me to sit, too.

"It's just that ... I don't know ... I was sort of wondering if there was ever a time, like, you know, that you felt like you didn't want to adopt a baby."

The smile on Dad's face disappeared.

"You know what I mean, right? I mean say that Mom wanted to adopt a baby and you thought that adoption wasn't a good idea, which, you know, isn't a bad thing because not everybody ..." Now that I was saying it out loud, it sounded so stupid and I couldn't believe that I had worried about it ear-lier. "Never mind. Stupid question." I jumped off the bed.

But Dad grabbed my arm and pulled me back down beside him, kind of hard. "Macey, I always wanted a daughter exactly like you. Look at me." He took me by the shoulders. "I've loved you from the very first second I held you in my arms and I will *always* love you."

I stared down at my feet. I had hurt his feelings. But I didn't totally believe him. Who would ever dream of having a daughter with skin that wasn't white and smooth like Deena's or dark and beautiful like Ty's but instead a mottled shade of brown, like a mud stain on a clean shirt, with nine fingers and gangly arms and legs and hair that springs up wildly all over her head? No one ever dreams of having a daughter like that.

"Mace?"

"I'm sorry. I started to wonder about it because ... well, because Grandma said today that you didn't want to adopt me."

Dad's body tensed up and he clenched his jaw for a second. "Macey, you know that you can't listen to Grandma, right? She's old and she's not well and sometimes she's—"

"Mean."

"Well, yes," Dad sighed, "sometimes she's mean."

"She told Eugene he was fat."

"Eugene went to Grandma's?!" Dad asked.

"And she kept hitting him over the head with a fly-swatter."

Dad tried to look appalled, but a little snorting laugh escaped his throat.

"All he wanted was to use the bathroom, but she thought he was an intruder." Now I was laughing.

"Poor Eugene." Dad fell backward on the bed, his arm across his face. After a second, he let out a big sigh and glanced at me out of the corner of his eye. "It's not funny. We shouldn't laugh."

"No, you're right," I said. "It wasn't funny." But my stomach hurt from holding the laughter in.

"Let's go check on Deena." Dad stood up and pulled his Phillies cap low over his forehead.

We had stopped just in time. Once in a while, when I laugh too much, the laughing turns into crying and I can't stop it. I felt on the verge right then.

Our bedroom door was locked. "Deena, open up," Dad called.

Deena flipped the door open and jumped in bed, her back against the wall. "I'm reading," she said. "Is that okay?"

"Sure, it's okay. I just want to make sure everything's all right before I head out. You two aren't fighting or anything, are you?"

"Daaaaad!" we said in unison.

Deena jumped up and threw her arms around my neck. She gave me a big, sloppy kiss. "There. See?"

"And neither one of you ate any dinner."

"You're a worrywart." Deena put on her sweetest face. "You could leave us some money for ice cream. Then you wouldn't have to worry that we were hungry or anything while you're gone."

Dad laughed. He looked at his watch. "Well, okay."

Deena gave me a high five.

"But you have to leave now and make sure that you come right back. I don't like it when you're out while I'm gone. I'll call you when I get to the stadium. And I already checked with Mrs. Chen. She's home, so you can go over there if there's an emergency or you get scared."

"Dad! We're not going to be scared!" We finally managed to get Dad out the door after he gave us about one hundred lectures on staying safe. You'd think we were two-year-olds and he was leaving us for a year. Deena wiped the table while I finished drying the dishes. Ty ran across the alley to ask her mom if she could come with us for ice cream.

"Did you call home?" I asked Eugene.

"When you were upstairs," he said.

"Can you stay?"

"Everything's cool," he answered.

We walked the two blocks to Mick's and got cones. It was still light out, but the heat had gone out of the day. People were sweeping their front steps, spraying the hose over their flowerpots or just sitting out watching little kids ride their Big Wheels down the sidewalk. All the older kids were hanging out, too, and the line in Mick's was pretty long. Eugene was getting lots of stares. I recognized those stares, a long look followed by a knowing glance at a friend and then a snicker or two.

We ate the ice cream sitting on the curb outside the store. I'm glad we ate it there instead of at home. If we had taken it home, it would all have gone to waste. Even Eugene wouldn't have been able to finish his cone after what we saw.

8

We sat on the wall in front of our house for a little while, so we didn't see it right away, which was a good thing. It was so perfect out, and we were having a great time hanging together. Ty was at her funniest and Eugene was laughing hysterically at everything she did. The whole neighborhood was coming alive. People were sitting on their stoops or taking walks around the block, and every car that came down the street was vibrating with music. Summer nights are my favorite.

George P. and George R. turned the corner with Sammy, one of the counselors from their group home. They had ice-cream cones from Mick's, too.

"Hey, George P.," I called to him. "What flavor did you get?" Three Georges live in the group home, which is kind of weird. George P. is my favorite. George R. scares me sometimes because he always looks angry and he never talks.

George P. stopped in front of us. He stared at his hand for a few minutes. "Chocolate," he finally said. The ice cream was melting, running down the cone and dripping over his fist.

"Eat up, buddy," Sammy said. "Take some licks from the sides."

But George P. started shaking his head back and forth and he wouldn't stop.

Sammy put his arm around George P.'s shoulder. "Something scared him up the street there," Sammy said, pointing, "but I'm not sure what. He won't say."

"You can tell us, George P. We're friends, right?" Deena had some extra napkins and she slid off the wall and wiped the ice cream from his sticky fist. But George P. just kept on shaking his head.

"Okay, don't worry about it, buddy. We'll head on home," Sammy said. "Thanks for the napkins, Deena."

Just then Ryan and Zach flew around the corner on their bikes.

"Watch out, boys!" Sammy called, moving George R. out of the way just in time.

"Stupid retards," Zach said under his breath.

I jumped off the wall, but Ryan flipped his bike between me and Zach. "We're headed to Joe's to play capture the flag," Ryan said. "You guys want to come?"

"We can't." I stuffed my bad hand into my pocket. "Our dad's at the Phillies game and we gotta stay home all night."

"How about you, Ty?" Zach asked.

"Yeah, and Eugene, too, you can play," Deena added. "You guys don't have to stay here with us all night."

Zach made a weird snorting sound. It made me want to step on his face.

"Nah. I'm just going to stay here and hang out," Ty said.

"Me, too." Eugene was starting to sweat again.

"Nobody asked you to come anyway, fat kid." Zach stuck his finger right in Eugene's face.

Ryan pulled on his brother's shirt. "C'mon, knock it off."

"What?" Zach complained. "Like he could really play. Give me a break."

Eugene's shoulders slumped for the third time that day. I stood next to him, arm to arm, and I didn't even care that he was all sweaty.

"Looks like Niner's got a new boyfriend," Zach sang.

Ryan shot a quick glance at me, his face turning red. He twisted his hands back and forth over his handlebars. "Hey, maybe I can stop by later tonight, see what you guys are up to. Is that okay?"

"Sure," I said, positive that my face was burning, too.

They started to ride off, but Zach turned around on his bike. "Niner and Eugene," he yelled. "The freak and the blob. You guys could be the stars of a horror movie."

Deena started to run after him, her fists clenched, but he pedaled too fast. She swung at him, but he was out of reach. He laughed as he rode up the street. "You could move in that house with those retards," he called over his shoulder. "You'd fit right in."

"Run away, you big coward!" Deena taunted.

"He is such a jerk," Ty fumed. "I could kill him."

I had killed him already, in my head, several times, and that scared me. But Zach had a point. I am something of a freak. Not just because of the obvious stuff like my missing thumb. I'm a freak because of what goes on inside me, the dark, ugly thoughts that live in my brain. I can't seem to stop them from coming and there are more of them all the time. A picture of Zach riding out onto Levick Street and getting hit by car after car had just flashed through my mind. It just popped in there as he rode away. I don't know where it came from and I couldn't stop it. I closed my eyes and I opened my eyes. Either way, it didn't matter. I still saw a dead Zach. This is how I know that something is wrong inside of me. I worry that it's growing.

It's something that no one knows about but me.

Last week I dreamed about Mom. She was bleeding and hurt, lying all alone on the floor in a small, dirty room. I saw her through a window, but I didn't do anything to help her. "You shouldn't have left," I called, banging on the glass. "Now aren't you sorry?" She never looked at me. Afterward, I wasn't sure if it had been a dream or if I had imagined it while I was awake, staring at the ceiling in my dark bedroom.

"How could you stand there and let him say that?" Deena yelled at me, stomping her foot.

"Yeah," Ty piped in. "You're way too nice, Macey. You could've cursed at him or something."

I shrugged. Zach had said much worse. I'm not way too nice. I'm the opposite. But I couldn't tell them that. "Let's forget about it. I'm going inside to get a drink."

And that's when we saw it. Right by the door in front of the step. It was on the welcome mat, covering all the letters except for the *me* at the end. We all froze and nobody said anything for a minute.

"Disgusting," Ty finally croaked.

A dead robin with its wings all splayed open lay in front of us, its head strangely twisted to the side. Small black ants were crawling over its eyes and in and out of its open beak.

The ice cream in my stomach started to roll dangerously. I put my hand over my mouth.

"Oh, poor little bird," Deena crooned. She lifted the robin and cradled its limp body in her small hands.

"Deena, that's gross! Put it down. Please!" Ty shuddered.

It was Eugene who noticed the writing chalked by the step. He read aloud, "'Give it back, or else this could be you.'"

We all looked at each other.

"What's that mean?" Eugene asked.

Ty shrugged. "I don't know. Maybe Zach did it when we were at Mick's."

I shook my head. "It wasn't Zach. I'm sure."

"How do you know?" Ty asked.

"Because. It was the guy from the bus stop," I blurted.

Deena's eyes got wide. "Maybe not, Macey. Maybe it was Zach. Remember the time he shot the squirrel with the BB gun?"

"Yeah, and he burns ants with a magnifying glass," Ty added. "This is so Zach."

I could be obsessing. But I had one of those creepy feelings. And ever since he had jumped at me at the window, I couldn't get rid of it. It was like I had been dipped in something slimy that wouldn't wash off. I looked over my shoulder and up the street. I didn't see him, but he could have been there. It felt like he was there. He could have been watching us to see what we would do. I felt shivery, like those ants were crawling on me. "It wasn't Zach," I repeated, surer of myself this time. I just knew.

"Yeah, but if it was that guy, Macey, why would he say 'give it back'?" Ty asked, pointing to the chalked words. "It's not like you have anything of his."

"I don't have anything of Zach's either," I reasoned.

"Yes you do," Deena reminded me. "You have his old base-ball glove."

"But that was last summer. Besides, he doesn't even know I was the one who stole it." Zach had thrown one of Deena's books down the sewer, and I took his glove the next day when he wasn't paying attention. I was gonna give it back eventu-ally, but I never did. It's still in the basement on a shelf some-where.

"Yeah, well maybe he finally figured out it was you."

"No, it's not Zach," I insisted. "It's that creepy guy. I know it." I stared at the words on the step. *Give it back.* My hand flew to my empty pocket. I stared at Deena. "The necklace," I finally said. "He wants the necklace."

"No way. That's so stupid. Why would a guy like that want a necklace with a locket on it?"

"I don't know! But that's what he wants." Ty and Eugene looked at me like I was crazy. Deena seemed more interested in the dead bird than in what I was trying to tell her. "Deena! Remember how you were mad because I wouldn't share what I found on the lawn? You were telling Mrs. Fitz and that's when he turned to stare at me, remember?" I could see his face all over again, the way he narrowed his small eyes and the way his lips disappeared into the dirty blond stubble on his face.

"That doesn't make any sense," Eugene said. "If it was his locket, why didn't he just ask you for it?"

"Yeah, he didn't have to go killing a bird." Ty shuddered again. "He could have just said that he lost it and it was his."

"Maybe he didn't kill it." Deena stroked the bird's head. "Maybe a cat did it."

"Right," Ty said, rolling her eyes. "A cat that knows how to spell and write with blue chalk."

"It's not his necklace, anyway," I blurted. "It's *mine*! She left it there for *me*." I stared defiantly at Deena, waiting for her to disagree with me. I was ready to explode when she did. But she just kept smoothing the feathers of that dead bird.

The phone rang and we all jumped. I carefully stepped over the feathers on the welcome mat, rushed inside, and picked up the receiver.

"Hello?"

"Mace?"

"Hey, Dad."

"Why are you out of breath?"

"No reason. We were sitting on the front steps and I ran to get the phone."

"Everything all right?"

"Sure, fine," I lied.

"You call me if you need anything, okay, baby?"

"Okay."

"And go inside soon. I don't want you outside when it's dark."

"Okay. I love you, Dad."

"I love you, too."

I waited until he hung up and then I talked quietly into the dead phone. "I wish you were home. I wish you would come home right now. I wish Mom was here, too." I held the receiver to my ear for a few moments, listening to the silence, then slowly clicked the phone back into its cradle. I couldn't remember what Mom's voice sounded like. If she called me right now, would I recognize her on the phone?

I walked to the bookcase and reached my hand behind the row of dusty cookbooks. I pulled out an old Magic Tree House paperback and found the photo of Mom that I stuck inside on page twenty-three. Deena had taken down the family portrait that used to hang on the wall next to our school photos, and she refused to tell Dad or me where it was. I think she threw it away.

This photograph was from the picnic we had at Pennypack Park last summer. Mom is down by the creek, and she's a little bit tilted, her left arm outstretched, leaning against a tree. I wish we had more pictures. I wish that we had a close-up of her face. She has a small birthmark shaped like a crescent moon, but now I can't remember which cheek it's on. She's too far away in the picture for me to tell. I can't believe that I've forgotten already. I can't see if she's smiling or not, either, but I think that she is. It was later that she cried.

She was unpacking the lunches when I screamed. Deena was chasing me and I slid into a bush that had a bees' nest in it. I got stung about fifty times and it felt like my leg was on fire. They had to rush me to the hospital, leaving all the sandwiches and snacks behind for the ants. Mom sat in the back seat of the car with me and I cried into her yellow blouse. She held my head to her chest and sang me a song the whole way. When we got to Nazareth Hospital, the nurse there asked a bunch of questions from a paper on her clipboard. They seemed to go on and on.

"Does she have asthma?"

"No," Mom answered.

"Any allergies? Any family history of—"

"No. Well, maybe. We don't know exactly. ..."

"Can't we skip this part?" I begged. "I don't have any family history. It's just me." I was only trying to be helpful. It wasn't the first time I had heard those questions and I wanted them to stop. My leg was growing fatter by the minute.

"Sweetie," Mom said, "you have a family history. You have Dad and me."

Dad leaned over and kissed my forehead.

"I know. I *know*. I just don't have the other kind of family history, like what Deena has. I don't have things that run in the family, like diseases and blue eyes." And light skin and shiny straight hair and good math grades. I wanted the doctor to come quick. I wanted to get this over with. I started crying.

Mom stood up and left the room without a word. There

was a long silence. The nurse looked uncomfortable and fiddled with the papers on her clipboard. Even though my leg was burning, the rest of me suddenly went cold. Mom hates any suggestion that I'm not completely part of the family, as much a daughter as Deena in every way. I'd seen her yell at store clerks and acquaintances and people in restaurants who made rude comments about me. But this was different, wasn't it? It was medical. I didn't mean anything more than that. I began to shake uncontrollably. The nurse ran to get a warm blanket.

Dad dropped into the seat that Mom had just left and put his arm around me. "I'm sure she's just checking on Deena in the waiting room," Dad lied. "She'll be right back."

But she never did come back. It seemed like it took five hours, but I finally got a shot from the doctor and some cream to rub over my stings. After a few days, my leg was back to normal. But Mom got sadder and sadder day after day. Deena and I tried to be extra helpful around the house and we were careful never to fight or complain when she was around. Sometimes, Mom spent the whole day in her bedroom. I wished there was a special cream for her, too—rub in three times a day and feel happier in a week.

I slid the picture back between the pages and dropped the book into its hiding place. I stared at the dusty cookbooks, unopened for almost a year. I needed to try to find my real family. The thought sliced through me, hot and painful. My *real* family. Maybe I belonged somewhere else all along. Maybe Mom would come back if I left. It was an ugly thought, but there it was. I raced upstairs to the bathroom and slammed the door. I slumped on the edge of the tub, suddenly exhausted. I wished everyone were gone and I could spend the night alone lying flat against the cool blue tiles, listening to the quiet drip of the faucet and staring up at the small patch of dark sky visible through the overhead transom window. I tried it, stretching out on the floor and crossing my arms like a mummy, wanting to sleep like one, to clear every last thought from my pounding head. But within a minute Deena was calling me, and I heard the stamp of feet through the house. I lingered for a few moments in the pale darkness, then forced myself up. I stared into the small mirror above the sink. My face was nothing more than a murky shadow, the outline of my wild hair the only thing that stood out in the dim light. I felt like a ghost, empty and aching, not sure where I belonged. Deena screamed for me again, an edge to her voice this time. I splashed cold water on my face and headed down to the living room.

Ty was on the couch. "They're in the basement," she said, "putting away the shovel. They buried the bird. Disgusting."

I grabbed a pot full of water and a scrub brush and erased the chalked threat from the front step. It was the time of day that reminds me most of myself, halfway between the light and the dark. Lamps were flicking on in the houses across the street and the air was getting cooler. I glanced nervously up and down the block but saw nothing suspicious. We all met back in the living room. I drew the curtains and we sat in the gathering darkness.

We were in a circle, talking about what we should do. Ty thought we should call the police. "That guy could be dangerous," she argued. "Besides, calling the police could be fun, too. Maybe we could get on *Action News*! That would be way cool."

Eugene was dead set against the police, but he didn't say why. "You should call your dad and ask him to come home. You've got to tell him everything. He's your dad. He'll know what to do."

"What do you think, Macey?" Ty asked.

"I don't know," I said, biting my thumbnail. "Let me think." I couldn't make up my mind. I needed more time for my slow brain to go through all the options. I was going to argue against the *Action News* thing, but then it occurred to me that it could be helpful. What if my birth mother was watching TV and she saw me? She would know where to find me. That made me excited and scared, too.

"Are you going to say something or not?" Deena asked me.

My brain was frozen with indecision. "You go next," I suggested.

Deena sighed. "Okay. We can't call the police or tell my dad."

"Oh, come on!" Ty complained. "Why not?"

Deena turned to me. "When's the last time that Dad went anywhere without us since Mom's been gone?"

That was easy. "This is the first time."

"Right. So what happens if he thinks we were in trouble the very first time he went somewhere? He'll never go out again! Besides, we'll be stuck in the house for the whole rest of the summer, or worse, he'll make us hang out at Grandma's house. Do you want that?"

I had to agree with her. Dad would be worried sick. He would watch over us every second that he was home and he wouldn't let us out at all when he was at work. He might even try to get us into that summer camp at the playground that we talked him out of once before. We're practically old enough to be the counselors. No way we want to spend our summer making straw baskets and having juice and pretzel snacks.

"I can't believe that you're giving up your chance to be on *Action News*." Ty seemed disappointed.

Eugene shook his head. "So what are you going to do, nothing?"

"Of course not," Deena retorted. "We'll just give him the necklace back."

"It's not his, Deena," I argued. "It's mine." I felt a lump growing in my throat.

"I know, Macey. I'm sorry. But why else would he want it if it didn't used to be his?"

I felt the first tears pooling in my eyes and I blinked them back. "Maybe because it's gold and it's worth money." But she was right. What choice did we have? I didn't want to upset Dad.

"It's broken, Macey. It can't be worth much money."

"Fine," I said. "We'll give it to him."

"Where is it?" Ty asked. "Can I see this crazy necklace that's causing all the problems?"

Eugene glanced at me and then dropped his eyes to his lap real quick.

"It's not here," I answered.

"Well, where is it?"

Deena looked at me. Even though the room was dark now, I could tell that her face was getting red. "Our grandma has it," she said.

"Oh, *greeeaaat*," Ty moaned.

"We have to go get it." Deena stood up.

"We?" Ty asked.

"Well, you don't have to come if you don't want to, but the rest of us are going."

I switched on the television to check out the Phillies game and saw that they were winning 2–0 in the top of the third. We had six more innings before Dad would leave for home. Deena called Dad on his cell to check in and ask if he was having a good time. She told him we were watching TV and playing board games and that everything was fine.

"There," she said, hanging up the phone, "he probably won't call us now for a couple of hours. We should be able to get the necklace and be back way before then."

We left the TV and the lights on inside. We closed all the windows, locked up the house, and stepped out into the dark street. Grandma's house was only five blocks away and all four of us were going. So why did I feel so creepy?

9

Plenty of people were still sitting out on their front steps, the tips of their cigarettes glowing in the dark. Most of the streetlights were working, and we walked in and out of the pools of yellow light. I was itching to run the whole way, but Eugene and Deena wouldn't be able to keep up and Ty would complain. She hates to run even though she's fast. We steered clear of some of the hangout corners where the older kids stood around. They drink and sometimes they throw their empty bottles at cars or smash them in the street. The police chase them away once in a while, but they always come back. A couple of times the cops have made drug arrests at the other end of our street. That scares Dad a lot.

When we got to Grandma's, we had an argument out front.

"I walked you guys here, but I'm not goin' in." Ty looked at Eugene. "Their grandma doesn't like me 'cause I'm black."

Eugene nodded. "She doesn't like me because I'm fat. She hit me over the head about fifty times already today."

"She doesn't like me because—" I wasn't really sure, but I had lots of theories. "—because I'm adopted and also my skin is not—"

"Macey!" Deena yelled. "That is not true! Stop saying that stuff."

It is true, but Deena doesn't want to believe it. Some people are against adoption, pure and simple, and Grandma is one of them. Deena is too good to understand that. To her, we are one hundred percent sisters in every way and how we were born has nothing to do with anything. She's right, of course, but sometimes she can't see what it feels like on my side.

"She likes *you*, Deena," I said. "And besides, you're the one who showed it to her in the first place."

"Yeah, well, I'm not going in alone."

We played rock, paper, scissors, shoot and Ty was the loser. She groaned and crossed herself several times. "Why am I doin' this? She's *your* grandmother, Macey!"

Maybe so, but I always felt more like an unwelcome stranger than a granddaughter. That made me pretty even with Ty.

"Yeah, Macey," Deena added. "She's going to look out the window and see you and wonder why you're not comin' in. What am I supposed to say?"

"Tell her I'm at home. I'll wait for you by the back door so she doesn't see me," I said, hurrying away before anybody could argue with me anymore.

The alley is a narrow strip of driveway that runs between the rear of two blocks of row houses. Each house has a cellar door that is set back in a cavelike entrance the size of a really big closet. Eugene and I waited there, our backs against the stone walls. It was pitch-black dark. No one could see us and I felt safe. Looking back, it's kind of obvious that we couldn't have picked a worse place to wait. But in the beginning, I felt real pleased with myself. I liked it in there. It felt as if we were wrapped in a cocoon or floating in a space capsule far away from everybody and everything.

"Is your Grandma always mean?" Eugene asked. His voice sounded small and hushed in the little cave.

"Well, yeah, I guess so," I said. "Most of the time, anyway. But I don't know if it's all her fault. She had a stroke a long time ago and my dad says that sometimes that can change a person."

"My grandma was real nice."

"Did she live near you?"

Eugene took in a big breath, like he was trying to steady his voice. Maybe I shouldn't have asked.

"Yeah." He breathed the word out in a long rush of air. "She lived in the same trailer park." Another big breath. "We went to the movies a lot and played card games."

"She sounds nice." My eyes were getting used to the dark. I could see Eugene's outline. He was sitting with his head in his hands.

"She was. Lots of kids used to, you know, make fun of me 'cause I'm so fat and all. I know this sounds kind of weird, but my grandma was my best friend."

"I don't think it's weird," I said, even though it was a little bit. I could understand it, though, because I know what kids can be like sometimes. "I'm lucky," I told him, "because I've got Deena and she sticks up for me all the time. But most kids stare at my hand a lot and they're all grossed out if they have to touch it. My grandma pulls away from me if I accidentally touch her with it. I'm kind of used to it, though. I don't let it bother me anymore."

And then the weirdest thing happened. Eugene reached out in the dark and took hold of my four-fingered hand. He didn't say a word. He just held it. And he didn't get all shivery or grossed out, and he didn't jerk his hand away either. Then a second weird thing happened. Maybe it was because we were sitting there like that in the dark and he couldn't see my face, but I started telling him things that I never talk about with anybody.

"I don't know how I lost my thumb. Maybe it just wasn't there when I was born. Maybe it got cut off or something in an accident, but I hope not. It gets achy sometimes in the spot where it should be, so maybe it did get lost somehow because why would it ache if it wasn't ever there?"

"Am I hurting it now?" Eugene's arm went stiff for a moment.

"No, you're not hurting it at all."

We sat quiet for a while. There was a rumble of thunder off in the distance and an occasional flash of heat lightning.

"You know what, Eugene?" I said, leaning toward him.

Another flash lit up Eugene's face for half a second. It was a little scary because his head was right up close to mine and his cheeks were all red and beaded with sweat. I wonder now if it wasn't all sweat, if maybe he was crying. I think maybe he was.

I didn't even wait for him to answer. I lowered my voice to a whisper. "I've been thinking that I might try to find my birth parents, you know, and just meet them. Do you think that would be wrong?"

"Didn't you ever ask about them before?" Eugene squeezed my hand a little tighter.

I shook my head in the darkness. I thought about them sometimes, especially this last year since Mom left us. But I never asked. I have two reasons. First, I get afraid that my birth parents will be mad that I found them and will send me away *again*. Once was bad enough. Second, I didn't want Dad and Mom to think that I wasn't totally happy with them or that I wanted to go someplace else. It seemed almost like it would be an insult. And what if my birth parents did want me back and I didn't want to go? It was easier and safer not to ask. But now I wonder about it more. My throat started to hurt.

Eugene started squeezing my hand and tugging on me.

"What's the—" I started to ask. Then I saw him. Eugene and I jumped up. We tried to run, but he was blocking the only way out. I backed up against the cellar door, Eugene beside me, and rattled the knob. *Open, please be open*, I silently prayed, even though I knew it wouldn't be. Grandma's house is locked up tighter than a maximum security prison. I would have screamed, but my throat was all closed up and nothing was coming out.

"Did you get my message?" His icy voice was raspy and low.

I tried to nod, but my whole body was shaking. Eugene stepped in front of me.

"Get out of the way, fat boy." The man grabbed the front of Eugene's shirt and shoved him hard against the wall. Eugene slid to the ground with a small whimper.

I tried to get down next to Eugene, but the man stopped me. "Stand there and don't move."

He flicked his lighter on and held the flame in front of my face. I squinted and turned away, but I could feel the heat burning close to my skin. He finally pulled it away to light a cigarette. He took a long drag before he spoke. "Okay, kid. Where is it? I'm running out of patience."

"I ... I don't have it right now. I can get it tomorrow. I'll give it back. I didn't know it was yours. I promise I didn't. I thought my mom left—"

"You think you're funny, don't you?" He blew his smoke right in my face and I started coughing.

"No, really, it was a mistake," I begged.

He slammed his hand into my chest and pinned me flat up against the door. Tears stung my eyes.

"You know where Frank's Deli is in the Somerville shopping plaza?"

I could barely move, but I tried to nod.

"Good. Go out back. Behind the Dumpster there's a pipe sticking out of the wall with a white plastic cap on it. Take the cap off and put what you owe me in the pipe. It better be there tomorrow and you better not mess with me. You got it?"

Lightning flashed and I saw his bloodshot yellowed eyes and hollowed-out cheeks. He blew more smoke in my face and flicked his ashes in my direction. "You've got one day. That's it." He gave me one hard shove against the door and disappeared out of the alcove into the alley.

I slid down onto the ground next to Eugene. Neither one

of us spoke. We were both panting hard. I was rubbing my chest, but I couldn't get the feeling of his long, dirty fingers off my skin.

"You okay?" I finally croaked.

"I think so."

Lightning flashed again as the storm moved closer, and I saw blood running down the side of Eugene's head.

I started pounding on the cellar door. "Deena! Deena! Ty! Open up!"

The cellar light went on and I could hear Deena hurrying down the stairs. She was giving me her angry look through the security bars on the door window while she fumbled with the locks. I thought she wouldn't ever get it open. I had never wanted to be inside Grandma's house so much in my whole life.

"Hurry up! Hurry up!" I shouted to her, my voice all high-pitched and shaky.

"Are you crazy?" she yelled when she had undone the thousand bolts. "Do you want Grandma to—" She shut up when she saw Eugene's head. "What happened?"

"He came. Let me in."

"Who?"

"The guy. The guy. The guy who wants the locket! He was here in the alley. He knocked Eugene against the wall. Will you get out of the way and let us inside?" Deena was still standing in the doorway.

"He pinned me—" I lifted my hand to my chest and that's when I lost it.

Deena pulled Eugene and me inside. Grandma's cellar is old

and creepy. It smells like earth and damp, and the one bare light bulb in the middle of the room throws long shadows over everything.

Deena pushed a trunk and box toward us. "Sit down," she said. "I'm sorry."

But I couldn't sit down. The trunk and box were probably full of spiders anyway. I paced back and forth across the concrete floor. "I just want to go home," I insisted. "Get Ty."

"Deena!" Ty called from the top of the stairs. "I ain't stayin' up here by myself, girl! What's goin' on?"

"Ty, bring me some wet paper towels, okay?"

"I want to go home, Deena." I was thinking only of myself once again. "I want to go home, *now.*"

"We are," she answered. "But Eugene's got a big cut. Hold on."

Ty came back with the paper towels and let out a long whistle. She handed them to Eugene. "What happened?"

He told them everything while he gingerly dabbed at the wound and wiped the dripping blood from the side of his face.

A loud clap of thunder made us all jump. Eugene went silent and we stared at each other and did nothing but listen for any strange noises. Was it really just thunder? I felt like I was having a heart attack.

I heard the familiar clump-drag-clump of Grandma's walker above my head.

"We better get out of here," Deena said.

"Did you get the locket?" I asked, heading for the stairs.

"You and Eugene better go out the back door."

"I don't want to go out in that alley. I want to go out the front."

"If you go upstairs, you'll get stuck. Grandma's already upset and afraid about the storm that's coming and—"

"Yeah, and about how I'm ruining her neighborhood," Ty added.

"Ty, she doesn't mean that stuff. She's old and confused," Deena said.

Ty snorted.

"Deeeeena! Where are you? What's going on down there?" Grandma shrieked.

"Nothing!" Deena held her finger to her lips. "I'm just making sure everything is all locked up down here for you."

Deena was shooing Eugene and me toward the cellar door.

"Hurry up!" Grandma called. "Are you watching that friend of yours? I have some good stuff in the basement."

"See what I mean?" Ty whispered.

"She thinks everybody's trying to steal from her," Deena insisted.

"Deeeeena!"

"Grandma, I'm *coming*!" Deena turned to me. "I'll meet you out front. Stand right under the streetlight. You'll be safe."

Eugene moved pretty fast for such a fat kid. But I was faster. I felt bad. I didn't want to leave him behind, but I couldn't slow my legs down and I flew out of that alley. Eugene and I huddled under the streetlight like it was some kind of force field protecting us from danger. Deena never answered me about whether she got the locket.

"What am I going to do if Deena didn't get the locket?" I asked. "That guy will kill me."

"She must have got it," Eugene said. "And if she didn't, you can come with me to Florida for a while and stay at my house until he forgets all about his stupid locket. He won't be able to find you there."

His face was clear in the streetlight. He really meant it. I didn't want to go to Florida, but Eugene's offer sure was nice. I know now that his offer was nothing short of amazing. Eugene didn't want to go to Florida either.

Ty came flying down the steps and joined us under the light. "She's coming. She's just saying good-bye and stuff."

Deena appeared a few seconds later.

"Did you get it?" I asked.

"I got it." She started to reach into her pocket.

"Not here!" I spat. "What if he's watching? I don't want him coming out."

Deena looked over her shoulder. "If he came, we could throw it at him and run away. Then it would be over with."

"No," I insisted. "I don't want to see him ever again in my whole life."

We headed for home, walking quickly and sticking close together. That's when the sky opened up and a soaking rain started to fall. We couldn't run because of Eugene and his cut head. He was feeling dizzy and we kept him between us in case he needed somebody to grab onto. He put his arm around my shoulder. Two bikes were racing toward us, splashing through the puddles in the street. One passed, but the other slowed and stopped. Ryan's mouth hung open for a second, then clamped shut in a tight line. His eyes bored into mine.

"Ryan!" I called to him. "We had to go to my grandma's house."

But he had already turned and pedaled away, and my words were lost in the noise of the storm. The rain was so bad that it had chased away all the druggies and the delinquents from the corner and we didn't have to make any detours around them. We were finally home. My hands were shaking as I slid the key into the lock.

10

"Quick, put on the Phillies game!" Deena ran upstairs to get towels for us.

"It's in a rain delay," Ty shouted up the steps.

I was rewinding the answering machine. One message. "Deena? Macey? Where are you guys? You're making me nervous. Call me."

"Oh no!" Deena cried, tossing us each a towel. "When did he call?"

I checked the machine. "Fifteen minutes ago."

She grabbed the phone and dialed. "Hey, Dad! Are you getting wet? ... Oh. Yeah, sorry. We were in the basement looking for a game to play and we didn't hear the phone ring. Macey just saw that the machine was blinking. ... Yeah. Everything's fine. You want to talk to Macey?"

I shook my head violently. I am not a good liar, especially when I'm all upset and shaky. I could never pull off what Deena was doing. I was ready to tell Dad everything. I wanted him to come home.

"Macey!" Deena yelled. "Oh, sorry, Dad. She's in the bathroom. Do you want to wait? Okay. I'll tell her. I love you, too."

She hung up the phone. "Dad says to tell you he called and he loves you."

I lent Ty some dry clothes, but finding something for Eugene was going to be a problem. I rifled through Dad's closet, even though I thought it was hopeless. Dad's not big and he sure isn't fat. I did find an oversized T-shirt that might work, but Eugene would never fit into any of Dad's shorts. It made no sense, but I drifted over to Mom's bureau. I checked to make sure Deena wasn't around and then I opened the drawers. I pulled out a sweater and held it to my face. Until she was gone, I never noticed that she had a certain smell. And then I would catch a whiff of it at unexpected times—pulling a blanket down from the shelf, hanging my coat next to hers in the closet, opening her jewelry box—and I would remember.

I inhaled deeply. This was the sweater she loved to wear in the fall. It had red and gold leaves stitched all down the front. She wore it when we took drives into Bucks County and stopped for apple picking at a farm. I remember sitting on her shoulders to reach for the low-hanging apples while she held tightly to my shins. She would cheer as I dropped each apple perfectly into the basket below. The farmer gave out free cups of cider, and we took a long hayride around the orchards. As the wagon rattled over the dirt road, she picked the straw out of my wild hair and kissed the top of my head. "I love you," she said. Why hasn't she come back? Wouldn't love make you want to come back?

"Macey!"

I jumped and knocked my knee into the dresser.

"What are you doing?" Deena asked.

"Just looking for something for Eugene to wear," I said guiltily, sliding the sweater back into the drawer.

"Yeah, right." She shook her head at me, but she wasn't mad. "Hurry up, okay?"

I brought Eugene the T-shirt and a sheet to wrap around his waist. It was the best I could do.

"We'll put the wet stuff in the dryer and it'll be ready in no time," I said.

But Eugene wouldn't take the sheet. He preferred his wet shorts. I threw our clothes in the dryer while Deena grabbed four sodas from the fridge and opened a bag of chips. We sat around the kitchen table with all the shades drawn and listened to the rain beat against the house.

"You should call the police," Ty argued. "I mean, I'm scared and I didn't even see the guy. Poor Macey."

I kept rubbing my chest where his hand had pinned me against the door. I could still feel the clamp of his fingers. "We should tell Dad now, Deena. He would want us to. And I'm scared."

"Macey's right," Eugene added. "There's something wrong with that guy. Did you see his eyes, Macey? They weren't right. They weren't normal."

Deena banged her glass down on the table. "Look, you guys aren't thinking right, okay? Do you know how much trouble that would cause? Dad would call the police and he would get all upset and we would have to stay in our rooms until we grew up and got married. And besides, Dad finally went out tonight. If we tell him, he'll never go anywhere again. It's scary, but you've got to think of more than yourself, Macey."

"Deena, you wouldn't say that if you were the one who had a freaky guy pin you to the wall," Ty said.

Deena pointed her chip at Ty. "That's not true. I would say the same thing if it was me. I'm thinking of Macey, too, you know. If we tell, it'll get blown up into a real big thing. If we put the locket in the pipe tomorrow like he wants, it'll all be over and we won't ever have to deal with him again. Don't you see?"

"Where's the locket?" I asked.

"Here." Deena pulled it from her pocket and put it into my hand. "You hold onto it."

"It's dirty," I said, holding it up to the light.

"Yeah, well, Grandma had thrown it out. I found it in the bottom of her trash can. I didn't have time to clean it off. We're lucky that we even got it back."

"She threw it out?!" I couldn't believe it. As I stood up to go to the sink, I heard a pounding at the kitchen door followed by a *rap, rap, rap* on the window. My chair clattered to the floor, and Ty knocked her soda clear across the table. Nobody moved.

Rap, rap, rap. It came again. We were frozen in place. *Boom!* Another blast of thunder shook the house.

Bang. Bang. "Helloooo! Anybody in there?" came a voice over the din of the rain.

We all let out our breath as Ty jumped up to open the door for her dad. Mr. Munah is a huge man and he filled up the whole doorway. Water was streaming off his umbrella and down his coat, but he was laughing.

"Let's go, Ty," he said. "Your mother sent me to take you home in this storm."

He spoke English with an accent that I loved. It was musical, I thought. Or maybe I liked it so much because I liked him. Mr. Munah worked two jobs, but when he was free he always joined in our games in the street and had as good a time as any of the kids. And he always picked me first for his team.

"Come on in, Mr. Munah," Deena said.

"No, thank you, young lady. I won't. If I came in, I would bring in a river with me. And how are you tonight, Miss Macey?" he asked from the doorway. "Are you practicing your soccer kick like I taught you?"

"I've been practicing," I said. "My dad takes me down to the park a lot."

"Good, good." He nodded. "Someday I will come watch you play in the World Cup."

"I'm ready." Ty crouched under his umbrella. "See you guys tomorrow."

"Come as soon as you wake up," Deena said, closing the door after them.

I cleaned up the spilled soda while Deena went into the basement to check the clothes. "Do you think we're doing the right thing?" I asked Eugene.

"I don't know. She's probably right about the police, though. They'd ask a lot of questions and probably make you go down to the station or something. Maybe if we give him the necklace tomorrow it'll all be over." Eugene played with the chip bag, rolling the end open and closed. "Can I ask you a favor?"

"Sure."

"Well, since the weather's so bad and all and my aunt lives blocks away, do you think maybe I could sleep at your house tonight? I mean, I don't need a bed or anything. I could sleep on the floor or even in the basement."

"We have a spare room, but I'd have to ask my dad."

Eugene's eyes dropped to the floor. "But I'm sure Deena and I can convince him," I quickly added. "We're pretty good at that."

Relief filled Eugene's face, washing out the lines around his eyes and mouth as he smiled at me. I thought I knew so much. I was sure that Eugene wanted to sleep over because he was afraid to walk home in the dark after all that had happened that night. But that wasn't what Eugene was afraid of.

"Will your aunt let you stay?" I asked. "She doesn't even know us."

"Probably," Eugene answered. "I'm pretty good at convincing, too."

Dad called to say that he was on his way home. The rain delay was going on too long for somebody who had to get up early for work in the morning.

Deena and I took turns showering and we finally persuaded Eugene to take one, too. While he was up there, Dad came home. He was drenched. His T-shirt clung to his chest and his shoes squished when he walked.

"Was it fun?" Deena asked. We were on the couch watching TV. We had worked out a plan to convince him to let Eugene stay over.

"Yeah, it was great," Dad said. "But I missed my girls. Come here. Give me a hug." He made a lunge for Deena and she squealed, twisting away.

I was squished, trapped in the corner of the couch. Dad stood over us and shook his head, spraying us with raindrops.

"Daaaaad!" We both yelled. "Stop!"

"Okay." He laughed. "I'm going to run up and take a shower."

"You can't," I said. "Eugene's up there." Our house has only one bathroom.

"Eugene!" Dad cried. "What's he doing in the shower?"

"We told him he should stay over at our house tonight."

"What?"

Deena put on her most innocent face. "Well, Dad," she explained, "we couldn't exactly make him walk home in this storm. It's been raining real hard for a long time and there was a lot of lightning, too."

Dad cocked his head and shot a glance at me. I looked down at my hands. "I can give him a ride home if he needs one," Dad offered.

"It's too late," Deena shot back. "He's staying with his aunt. She went to bed at nine o'clock and Eugene doesn't have a key."

"You've got this all worked out, haven't you?" Dad asked.

Deena didn't even crack a smile. I pretended to be absorbed in the television even though it was just a commercial.

"Well, I'd like to talk to Eugene about this," Dad said, his voice softening.

"Good luck," Deena complained. "He's been up there for about an hour."

"I think he might be afraid to come out. I gave him one of your T-shirts to wear, Dad, but I couldn't find any pants that would be his size." I kept my voice low. "I gave him a sheet."

"A sheet?!" Dad shook his head. "Oh, Macey. That's terrible. I'll find something." And Dad squished up the steps.

Later, it took a lot of begging, but we finally got Eugene to come downstairs. He was wearing an old pair of red bathing trunks and a clean T-shirt that stretched across his belly and hung down almost as long as the trunks. Even though she had promised she wouldn't, Deena laughed so hard that she rolled off the couch and fell onto the floor.

"I'm sorry. I'm sorry," she giggled from the carpet. "You look like you're going to the beach or something."

I'm sure that Deena made that up to keep herself from saying something worse. His arms and legs were so pale and puffy that he looked like a giant marshmallow man, except that his face was now turning as red as the trunks.

Dad gave Deena one of his looks. She got up and brought Eugene a bowl of popcorn and a glass of soda.

Dad gave him the third degree. "And you're sure it's all right with your aunt?" Dad asked for the fourth time.

"Yes, sir," Eugene answered. "I gave her your address and phone number. But I could go home, if you wanted. I'm sure if I knocked long enough, I could wake her up and she would let me in. She usually doesn't go to bed this early, but she hasn't been feeling well all week."

Those last two lines were a stroke of genius. I stared at Eugene in awe. His face was blank. I wondered how hard it was for him to keep it that way. For the first time, I realized that Eugene was hiding something. He hadn't called anybody to ask permission. We were together all night except for when I went up to get him some dry clothes. And he never asked to use the phone.

Dad was quiet, rubbing his chin and thinking.

"I could call her again," Eugene offered. "She doesn't have a phone in her bedroom, but I could try her cell number. Sometimes she leaves her cell phone on the nightstand."

"Where does she live?" Dad asked.

"3409 Aldine Steet."

"And what's her phone number?"

Eugene rattled off both her home and cell numbers and Dad wrote them down on a pad.

"Well," he said, "I'm not real happy about this, but I also don't want to wake up a sick lady at this hour. I just wish I had been here when you called her."

"*We* were here, Dad," Deena lied. "Don't be so fussy."

Dad sighed. "All right. At least I have some numbers here in case I need to call her for any reason. What's her name?"

"Jean Wilson," Eugene answered.

Summer nights are the best. The rain had stopped and we opened up all the windows. We had the TV on low, but mostly we just talked and laughed about stuff. I'd be lying if

I said that I was totally relaxed. I thought a bunch of times about whether to tell Dad about what happened. The words were on the tip of my tongue. But everything felt safe and okay with Dad there, and it was easy to believe what Deena had said about the whole thing being done and over with by tomorrow. Besides, I could tell how much fun Dad had had hanging out with his friends from work. He told us all about the game and the people who were sitting around him and the funny things that they did. One boy a row down from Dad was there to celebrate his twelfth birthday with his father, and the boy was so desperate to catch a fly ball that he jumped out of his seat in anticipation every time he heard the crack of a bat. Before the boy went to the men's room with his father, he asked Dad to hold his glove till he got back. Dad ran out to the merchandise stand and bought a baseball. When the boy came back to his seat, Dad told an exciting story about how Ryan Howard had hit a towering pop fly and it landed, *plop*, right in the boy's glove. And all the people in the seats nearby insisted that it was true, even some who had been making fun of the kid earlier.

"My dad was a big baseball star at Baker High School, and he could've made it to the major leagues if he hadn't gotten hurt," I told Eugene.

"Macey," Dad intoned. "Eugene doesn't want to hear about ancient history."

It's true, though. He still holds the record for strikeouts in a single season. And they have his name on a banner in the gym and on trophies in the case in the main hallway. Mom took Deena and me to see them one time. She was really proud of his records, even though she didn't know him back then. But he got hurt in his senior year. He ripped an important muscle in his shoulder and he couldn't pitch right after that. Colleges stopped calling him, and his hopes for a scholarship disappeared. Since his dad was dead and he had two younger brothers, he went right to work after he graduated.

"Is Baker High around here?" Eugene asked.

"Yeah," I said. For a minute I thought that Eugene might want to go see the trophies, but that was stupid of me.

"I think my aunt might have gone there."

"Her name does ring a bell," Dad said. "Maybe I know her."

Eugene immediately perked up. Dad has lived in this neighborhood his whole life and he knows an awful lot of people. Sometimes he talks about getting out because it's not the safest place to live anymore, but I think that it would be hard for him to leave, especially since nobody else could take care of Grandma and we don't want to think about bringing her along to live with us. Maybe I'm selfish, but I like it better when she has her own house. And I don't want to move anyway. Deena and me know how to stay safe. We avoid the bad corners and the bad people and we stick close to the house after dark. Mom was in favor of moving. When you think about it, that's what she ended up doing. She just didn't wait for the rest of us.

Dad was listing the people he knew who had the same last name as Eugene's aunt. He wasn't sure if he knew her because *Wilson* was such a common last name and Eugene wasn't too good at describing her looks. But she was probably the sister of a guy who used to work with Dad or the teller at the PNC Bank or a girl he knew from high school who was on the tennis team.

Eugene was really disappointed that his aunt had such a common name. It seemed silly at the time, but now I know why. He was more than disappointed. He was at a dead end. And that's probably why he decided to trust me that night.

11

We found an old fan in the basement and got Eugene all set up in the guest room. I couldn't sleep. I keep an old knit shirt of Mom's in my bed to sleep with, but it wasn't comforting me. I kept seeing yellow eyes and feeling the pressure of a hand against my chest.

"Hey, Deena," I whispered across the room. "Are you awake?"

"Yeah," she answered. "It's too hot to sleep."

That's what she said, but I think she was worried, too.

"Want to sleep on the floor?" I asked.

"Okay." She jumped up right away, and that's when I knew she was as nervous as me.

We laid the sheets and blankets between our beds. We did this a lot when we were younger and pretended that we were camping out. We had so much fun that we would go to bed extra early some nights. Mom would even let us have snacks in our room and gave us flashlights to play with. Dad would sneak in and scare us, acting like he was a bear after our food. Tonight, I was just happy to have Deena right there next to me. It made me feel safer.

"It'll be all right," Deena said. "You'll see. This time

tomorrow night we'll be all done."

I still had butterflies in my stomach. "Are you sure that we shouldn't tell Dad?"

She let out a big sigh. "We already decided, Macey. I'm sure. Trust me."

I do trust Deena. She's smart. Adults always made comments to Mom like, "She's so mature." Or "What a bright girl." Mom answered with a smile on her face, "Yes, well, she's ten going on twenty."

I lay in the dark and listened to the drone of the fan. From across the alley, I could smell the Chinese food that Mrs. Chen was cooking for her husband. When he works the late shift, she waits to have dinner until midnight.

After a while, I could tell by the sound of her wheezing that Deena had fallen asleep. Every breath came out with a funny little whistle. I got up and went to the window, leaned on the sill, and pressed my face to the screen. Across the alley I could see the Chens at their kitchen table, eating with chopsticks and talking. Mrs. Chen taught me to use chopsticks, and I'm pretty good at it. The smell was making me hungry. I could hear the traffic in the distance on Levick Street, the occasional slam of a car door, and Mr. Silas's dog barking and yapping. Mr. Kovitch was stumbling up the alley, headed home from Flannigan's, the bar on the corner of Bridge Street. I watched him drop his keys three times before he managed to open up his back door. Mom always made a low "tsk-tsk" sound when we saw him approaching us on the street, and she would only nod in response to his hellos. "Let that be a warning to you," she would say after he had passed. I wasn't sure if she was warning us against his peculiar smell or his funny walk until Deena filled me in on what a drunk was.

After Mr. Kovitch slammed his door, I heard a new noise coming from the window next to mine. My whole body tensed up and I pressed my ear against the screen. For a minute, I thought that I had imagined it, but then the faint sound came again. It was definitely there. The window next to mine was Eugene's. I tiptoed to my bedroom door and crept out into the hallway. Dad was snoring, alone, in his room. I listened at the lock on Eugene's door, and I was pretty convinced that he was crying very quietly.

I used one finger and did a faint *tap-tap* on his door. The sound inside stopped, but there was no answer. I cracked the door open. "Eugene," I whispered. "It's Macey. Can I come in?"

I took his silence as a yes and edged into the room. Eugene was a big mound under the sheets with his head sunk into the pillow. He was pretending to be asleep, but it wasn't dark enough for him to get away with it. Lots of our neighbors have security lights by their back doors, and they come on whenever anything passes close enough, even a cat or a dog. A big rectangle of light from the alley was shining through the window onto the ceiling above Eugene's bed. He peeked at me through one eye.

Mom used to sew in this room. I moved silently around the bed and pulled the stool out from under the sewing machine. "I can't sleep," I whispered, settling onto the stool.

Eugene gave up faking and turned his head toward me. "Me either."

"Is the bed okay?" I asked.

"Oh, yeah. It's fine."

"Do you want another pillow or anything? I probably should have given you two pillows."

"No. One's fine."

A siren wailed in the distance. I grabbed a box of tissues from the chest and put it on the bed next to Eugene. He took a few out, pulled the sheet over his head, and blew his nose. "Macey," he said between sniffs, "can I tell you something?"

"Sure." I have to admit that I wasn't really sure that I wanted to hear what he was going to say. He was still hiding under the sheet while he talked.

"You have to swear that you won't tell anybody."

It was weird swearing to a sheet, but I did. "I swear. Eugene, why don't you come out?"

He didn't answer, but I could tell he was shaking his head. "Macey, I got no place to live."

"What?" I couldn't have heard him right. The security light in the alley switched off and the room went dark.

Eugene slowly lowered the sheet till only his eyes showed. He was ghostly looking and he was scaring me.

"What are you talking about?" I asked. "You got a house in Florida, right? You said I could stay there. And you have an aunt in Philadelphia. You told my dad her name was Wilson or something."

The sheet went back up. "I can't find her."

"What do you mean you can't find her? You gave my dad her address."

A sigh came from under the sheet. He finally came out, sitting on the edge of the bed in Dad's old T-shirt and bathing trunks. The whole bed groaned when he moved. Eugene looked at me briefly, then hung his head. "Don't get the wrong idea or anything," he began. "But I sort of stole some money from my stepdad in Florida so that I could come here. I'm going to pay him back as soon as I can. I'm not a thief or anything," he quickly added.

"I used some for a bus ticket and some for a taxi to my aunt Jean's house. Only I didn't tell her I was coming, and when I got there the people in the house said that she didn't live there anymore. I never thought that she might've moved."

My mouth was wide open, but no words were coming out.

"She used to send me birthday presents." Eugene looked up at me. "You swore you wouldn't tell. Remember, you swore."

"I know. I know. I won't tell. But what are you going to do? How come you ran away from Florida?" I'm pretty sure that Eugene was older than me, but I don't think I could ever be brave enough to go that far all by myself. It must have been something bad.

"I don't know what I'm going to do, but I'm not going back. Not ever." Eugene's hands, resting on his puffy legs, had curled into tight fists.

I could tell that he was thinking about the reason he left, but he wasn't saying what it was. And I got to thinking while Eugene was clenching and unclenching his hands. Was Mom this angry, too? Did we do something so bad that she would never come back?

"Eugene," I asked, "did you tell them why you were leaving so they would know? They might really want to know."

He shook his head. His voice was flat. "They don't care. I promise."

"But what about your grandmother? She must miss you so much."

"They sold her trailer after my dad died and she's in a nursing home. I haven't seen her for a whole year." Eugene pulled his shirt up over his face. He didn't make a sound, but I could tell he was crying by the way his shoulders were shaking.

I moved closer and put my arm around his shoulder. We sat that way in silence for a few minutes. Deena pushed the door open. "Macey!" she hissed.

I jumped ten feet in the air and tripped over the sewing stool on my way down. She scared me so much I felt like I was having a panic attack. "Try to get some sleep," I croaked to Eugene, and I left him sitting on the side of the bed with his head in his shirt.

Deena grabbed the front of my pajama top and pulled me into our bedroom. "*What are you doing? Are you crazy?*"

"I wasn't doing anything." Deena reads too many books. She had the wrong idea. "I couldn't sleep. We were just talking."

Deena shook her head at me. She probably would have argued with me more, but she was wheezing too badly.

"Do you want to do the 'peep'?" I asked. The "peep" is the peak flow meter. Deena blows into it and it shows how her lungs are working. When Deena was little, she couldn't say it right and it has always been the "peep" since then. She nodded and we went downstairs together. I pulled the peep from the drawer, and Deena blew into it three times. Each time she came up way short of the marker that she was supposed to reach. I opened the closet and took out her nebulizer. I squirted the medicine into the cup and Deena strapped the mask over her nose. We sat on the couch with the TV on low while the machine pumped out the medicine in a foglike mist.

When I was little, I was jealous. I wanted to smoke the medicine, too. That's what I used to say. Besides the fact that it looked like fun, I wanted the attention that came with it. Deena would sit on Mom's lap as the machine worked and Mom would stroke Deena's hair and forehead. I hated being the healthy one then. Mom had asthma, too. It's something else she and Deena had in common. Something I couldn't understand. "You can't imagine what it feels like to not be able to breathe," Mom had said to me when I was pouting. Now, when I think of her, I truly can't breathe. It's like a giant weight sitting on my chest and pressing all the air out of my lungs.

Dad found us in the morning asleep on the couch with the TV on. He lifted Deena into his arms and carried her upstairs to bed. I was sitting up when he came back.

"I can give you a piggyback ride," he offered.

"That's okay." I smiled. I was too big to be carried in his arms.

He sat next to me on the couch. "Bad night for Deena? You should have gotten me up."

"No, it wasn't too bad. She was just wheezing a little."

"What was her peep?" Dad asked.

I showed him the little book where we keep a record of Deena's numbers. She has to take it with her whenever she goes to the doctor.

He sighed. "Maybe I should get another job and we should go live in a little house in the country somewhere where there's fresh air." He looked at me out of the corner of his eye. "I could be a farmer. What would you think of that?"

I laughed. "You'd be good with the tractors, but I think that I would have to milk the cows."

"And Deena could shear the sheep."

"She might be allergic to the wool," I reminded him.

"And the hay, too, for that matter. And the grass and the ragweed and the cows and the goats."

I was giggling now.

"Poor Deena. I guess we'll just stay here," Dad said. "That's the end of my farming career. How about some breakfast, or are you going back to bed?"

"I'll have breakfast. I'll make your coffee."

"Great." Dad kissed the top of my head. "I'll grab the paper."

I inhaled deeply as I scooped the coffee grounds into the paper filter. Dad won't let me drink coffee, but I sure love the smell of it. I could hear him on the front steps, talking and laughing while I poured the water into the machine and turned it on. Dad can't step one foot out of the house without running into people he knows. It always makes me feel proud when we're out and friends honk and wave at him as they drive by or people run across the street to shake his hand and clap him on the back. I set out a bowl for Dad's Cheerios.

"Thanks, baby," he said, sitting down with the paper.

He slid the comics across the table to me. I had a glass of chocolate milk and a couple of doughnuts.

"Mrs. Fitz says hi. She thinks I did such a good job fixing up the wall out front that she wants me to come by and fix hers, too."

"Ryan thought it looked good. He said so yesterday." I was still embarrassed that I hadn't noticed it before then. "Where was I when you did it? I would have helped."

"Hmmm?" Dad gets sucked into the paper in the mornings and doesn't always hear when you talk to him. The good thing is that I'm the best kid in my class at current events because Dad is always discussing what he reads. He tells me about tsunamis and Social Security and armed conflicts in Africa. I'm the only one in my class who knows that Castro's in Cuba and Putin runs Russia. The worst is the Middle East. He tries to explain the situation there, but I get very confused. Sometimes, it's like he's talking to himself. Charlie Brown and Woodstock are more my speed.

"Look at this," Dad mumbled. "Some guy got beaten up last night one block over on Rockland." He shook his head. "Can you believe this? The guy's in the hospital and he won't even cooperate with the police."

Dad pushed away the metro section in disgust and picked up the sports page. "Man Beaten," the headline read. The picture beneath it took my breath away. It was him. It was the man with the yellow eyes.

12

"Deena, wake up!" I pulled the pillow out from under her head and shook her again.

"Go *away!*" she pleaded.

"No, you have to come. It's important. It's life-or-death important. Come on."

She finally dragged herself out of bed and padded downstairs after me, rubbing her eyes and complaining the whole way. When we got to the kitchen, I slapped my hand on the metro page. "There. Read that."

Deena sunk into a chair, but her eyes were wide open now. "It's him," she said. "The guy from the bus stop."

"I know it's him! Now what do we do?"

"Wait. I'm still reading."

His name was Anthony Delladonna. Three men attacked him on Rockland Street at approximately 12:15 a.m. The attack was broken up by police who had been called by residents on Rockland who were awakened by the disturbance. The assailants ran from the scene and were still at large. Police believe that the victim knew his assailants, but he refused to name them or to give any descriptions. Delladonna had a broken right arm (the one he had used to hold me against the wall) and two broken ribs, received ten stitches to his forehead, and lost two teeth. It didn't mention his yellow eyes, but I saw them again and I shuddered.

Deena looked up from the paper. "Wow. That's so weird."

"Weird? It's scary!" I cried.

Deena neatly folded the paper and put her hands over his picture. "It's not our fault. It didn't have anything to do with us. We don't have to be scared."

I was already scared before this even happened. "How do you know the fight didn't have anything to do with the locket?"

"Oh, come on, Macey," Deena argued. "How many guys beat up another guy over a locket? It doesn't make any sense."

She was right. It didn't make any sense. But I was getting a bad feeling. I had a bad feeling the day that Deena went to the hospital, and I had a bad feeling that when Mom went on her trip she wasn't going to come back real soon like she promised. Mom didn't like it when I got a bad feeling about something. She said if I would use my brain and think things through logically, I would see that my bad feelings were silly. And sometimes they were. But how can I stop feelings from coming? They just pop into my head and my chest without warning. If Mom were here, I would ask her that. But I can't ask her because my feeling was right. She didn't come back.

I felt a tap on my shoulder blade, and I jumped forward and crashed my knee into the table leg.

"Sorry," Eugene said.

I dropped into a chair and rubbed my kneecap. How could I have not heard him walk up behind me? "It's all right. I'm kind of jumpy," I explained. "I didn't see you."

We showed Eugene the newspaper article, and I couldn't help wondering if maybe his mom was reading about him right now in his Florida hometown paper. "Overweight Boy Steals Money, Runs Away." Tomorrow's edition might say, "Found in Philadelphia with Nine-Fingered Adopted Girl." Me and Eugene, we could be in the Strange but True section of the news.

"That's him," Eugene said, looking up with wide eyes.

"No kidding, Sherlock." Deena pulled the paper away from him. "We already know that."

We ate breakfast in silence. I think we were all trying to figure out the best thing to do. I was starting to have some trouble keeping my doughnuts down, partly because of my nerves and partly from watching Eugene. He tried to be polite, but he was downing most of the box. Maybe he was hungry, but I wondered if he was stocking up because he didn't really know when he would eat again. I know that I swore not to tell, but I had to change his mind so that I could at least tell Dad. Dad would help him. Dad can help anybody.

There were two hard bangs on the back door, a short pause, then three quick taps. It was Ty. She has a special code so that we always know that it's her. Last year when Colin Whittaker was in love with Deena, he used to knock on the door at least ten times a day. We stopped answering in the hopes that he would give up and go away. That's when Ty developed her unique bang-tap routine.

"What's up, guys?" Ty asked, grabbing a powdered doughnut from the box. "You all look like you're going to a funeral or something."

We would be. But none of us knew that yet. I wonder if Ty gets feelings, too, and if she was having one right then.

Deena pushed the paper toward Ty without saying a word.

"'Water and Sewer Rates to Rise,'" Ty read. "So what? What is this?"

"No, stupid." Deena flipped the paper. "This story."

Ty squinted at the small print. "Okay. So somebody got beat up last night. I still don't get it."

"It's him," I said, remembering that Ty had never seen the guy. "It's the man who was at the bus stop, the man who grabbed me last night."

"No way!" Ty put her doughnut down and wiped her hands on her shorts. She read the article while we watched. "That's weird," she said when she had finished. "And creepy. What are we going to do now?"

"The same thing as we planned," Deena said. "We go and put the locket in the pipe and that will be the end of it."

"But what if somebody else takes it before he gets out of the hospital?" Eugene asked. "Maybe you should wait for a couple of days."

"Yeah, but we're not going to know when he gets out of the hospital. And besides, the pipe is probably his secret hiding spot. It's not like anybody else is going to know to look in it."

"Can I see the locket?" Ty asked.

I ran upstairs and pulled a tin box from under my bed. It

was filled with all of our treasures, and it was starting to look a little sad. A piece of velvet ribbon, a German coin, three postcards, an old-fashioned key, a single gold earring, two ten-dollar bills, a silver pen with initials engraved on it, a rabbit's foot, a clothespin doll, the locket, and the letters from Mom. I slid the last one out of its envelope and unfolded it. I reread the letters a lot, whenever Deena isn't looking. I can't help myself. I like to see Mom's handwriting, and I try to hear her voice in my head and picture her with the pen and paper as I read.

My dearest girls, it began, *I miss you so much and I cannot wait to see you again.* I ran my finger over the words on the page. They were real and she wrote them and she wouldn't lie. *Today I took over the lecture in Aunt Janice's class because she wasn't feeling well. It was exciting and I was so glad that I could be a help to her. After class, a number of students who had questions came up to me and called me "Professor." (Imagine that!)*

I *could* imagine Mom as a professor, teaching at a college like Aunt Janice. She is definitely smart enough. We have lots of colleges in Philadelphia, though, and I wonder why she never thought about that. I slid the letter back into its envelope before Deena started yelling for me to hurry up. I put the box back and ran down to the kitchen. I dropped the locket into Ty's hand.

"Okay," she said. "I don't get it. What's the big deal about this locket? It's broken. It's kind of lame, if you ask me."

Eugene took it from Ty. "It does look sort of beat-up. Maybe it has a special meaning to him, though. Maybe his girlfriend gave it to him."

"Yeah, maybe. But then how come he didn't just ask for it instead of acting all angry and creepy?" Ty asked.

"He's not normal," I told them. "You have to see his eyes to know what I mean."

"We'll take it up to Rollins Jewelry Store," Deena suggested. "We'll tell them we found it and say that we were wondering how much it was worth. They'll know if it's rare or something."

Our plans were set. I hurried upstairs to change. As I passed the spare room, I noticed that Eugene had neatly made the bed and arranged the decorative pillows in the exact places they had been. His wet shorts from last night were hanging on a chair in front of the fan. I thought I would check if they were dry. When I picked them up, I felt something in the back pocket and I slipped my hand in to see what it was. It was Eugene's wallet. I should have put it right back, but I didn't. I admit that I was nosy, poking around in something that was none of my business. The money he had stolen was damp but lined up carefully in the billfold. I flipped through the photos. There was Eugene and his grandmother sitting at a small table with a deck of cards dealt out in front of them; Eugene and his parents standing in front of a trailer; his father, a very large man with tree-trunk legs and a round, smiling face, leaning against a pickup truck and proudly holding up a fish with his right arm.

"Hey," Eugene said from behind me.

I felt the blood rush to my face. "Eugene, I'm sorry. I just … I was gonna put your shorts in the dryer and …" I'm not a good liar, so I gave up.

Eugene didn't say a word. He stood beside me and looked down at the photo. He took the wallet out of my hand, closed it up, and stuffed it back into his pocket. I felt like a criminal. That's why I opened the drawer of the sewing-machine table and took out a picture of my own. I wanted to even things up between Eugene and me. "This is my mom," I said, handing him the photo.

It was Christmas and she was sitting on the couch with a small box in her hand and a big smile on her face. I had made her some scented soaps with a kit that I had bought. She was allergic to them, though, and when she used them that night in the bathtub, she got a rash all over her body and she wheezed for a whole day and a half. The next year I bought her a chocolate reindeer. Even Deena's not allergic to chocolate.

Eugene stared. "She looks nice," he said. "Where is she anyway?"

I paused. It's the question I ask myself every day. "I don't know," I finally answered. "She went on a trip last year to visit her sister in Ohio, but she hasn't come back yet."

"How come?"

"Well, she ... my aunt Janice says she went on another trip, somewhere west, because she needs some time and space." I tried to make it all sound so normal and regular—an ordinary leave of absence, kind of like when Dad went on a golf trip with his friends a few years ago. Only she didn't take any golf clubs or any friends either. "She's coming back," I added bravely, "just as soon as she's done."

Eugene looked up at me from the picture. "As soon as she's done what?"

I suddenly felt incredibly embarrassed, like I was standing there in front of Eugene without any clothes on. I snatched the photo from his hand and turned my back on him. It wasn't fair, but I couldn't help it. I wished I had never met Eugene. I wished he was out of my house.

"Did I say something wrong?" he asked.

I was too mad to answer. I heard him whisper "sorry" before I slammed the door on my way out.

I kicked my own bedroom door shut. I gripped the photo and ripped it over and over until it was nothing more than shiny pieces of confetti. I pulled the tin box out from under my bed and grabbed the top letter. I tore up the envelope and the stamp and all four pages of her handwriting. I tore up her glorious college lecture and all her excitement at being called "Professor." I tore up her promises of how she couldn't wait to see us again. I tore up "Love Forever, Mom." And when the pieces were all so small that I couldn't tear them any further, I stomped them into the floor. It was all a lie. I buried my face in my pillow.

I'm not sure why Eugene's questions got me so upset. "As soon as she's done what?" he had said. And I didn't know. It was like a slap in the face, a bucket of cold water over my head. What could she be doing that was more important than coming home to Dad and Deena and me? And why couldn't she at least call to let us know?

I was so mad at Eugene. It wasn't his fault, but for some

weird reason, that made me even madder. He must have heard me having a fit. I'm usually not like that, but it felt like I was going to explode and I couldn't keep it all inside. How could she not even send us a Christmas card? I threw things across the room, my soccer trophy, my piggy bank, a deck of cards. And when I didn't have anything left to throw, I punched the wall with my fists. When I ran out of energy, I threw myself across my unmade bed. I didn't see Eugene carefully folding the clothes Dad had lent him and neatly piling them on the chair. I didn't hear him move quietly down the stairs or softly close the front door behind him.

When Deena came upstairs to find me still pouting fifteen minutes later, Eugene was gone. I had never asked him why he stole the money or why he ran away. He was in a strange city all by himself and he didn't even have anywhere to sleep. I should have been feeling guilty and worried for him. But all I could feel was mad and there wasn't room for anything else.

13

Deena offered to let me carry the locket to the jeweler's, but I refused. She had found me on the bed with the bits of paper scattered all over the room and she had cleaned everything up without asking me a single question or acting angry. She should have been mad. The letters and photos were hers, too. I didn't have any right to destroy them.

"Let's go get a drink," she said in a real soft voice, like a mother to a baby. She was worried about me. I didn't answer, but I pushed myself off the bed and pounded down the steps after her into the kitchen.

"I'll carry the locket," Ty offered. "This stupid locket is makin' everybody act real weird."

"Turn it over," I ordered. "See the numbers inside?"

Ty cradled the small heart in her palm. "Oh, yeah. I see them."

"It's my mom's birthday," I said, trying to keep my voice real even. "I thought ... I thought ..." I gave up trying to explain. It wasn't worth it and I didn't even know what I thought anymore. I shot a warning look at Deena in case she had any ideas about making fun of my silly hopes, my grasping at every little thing as some sort of sign that Mom was coming back. It was all so plain now how stupid I had been.

We were in the kitchen, at the table, and Deena got up and left. She had a habit of doing that whenever it looked like a discussion about Mom was coming. Ty looked at me. "You thought it was your mom's, right?"

I put my head in my hands and nodded.

"Maybe it was, Macey. Like you said, it's got her birth date in it and all. Maybe she ..."

"Don't, Ty," I interrupted. "I don't even want to talk about her, or I'll just get upset in front of you."

"So what? I don't care. Get upset. There's nothin' wrong with that. My mom still cries whenever she talks about my grandma."

"Why? What happened?" I asked. Ty's parents grew up in Liberia, in Africa. They immigrated to America before Ty was born. Ty's done lots of reports on Liberia and given at least two class presentations that I can remember. But I don't remember anything about her grandma.

"There was a war going on when my parents escaped to here. After they left, my mom never saw her mother again," Ty said in a hushed voice.

I shook my head. "It's not the same, Ty." And then I said it. "Moms aren't supposed to leave their kids behind." That was one of the thoughts that was brewing for a long time in the volcano deep inside me. But anytime it tried to come up, I pushed it right back down. Now it was out with no way for me to put it back and pretend I wasn't thinking about it. And

I didn't care. "Your mother wouldn't have left you in Liberia, would she?" I demanded.

"No," Ty admitted. "I guess she wouldn't."

Ty and I sat quietly staring at the table. My face was burning. I got up and took a long drink of cold water. As mad as I was, I couldn't shake the feeling that I drove Mom away like I drove Deena out of the kitchen and Eugene out of the house. Dad is so patient and friendly and nice, you can't help but love him. And Deena is the perfect daughter, the kind that every mom would want. She's so smart in school and she's organized and neat. She never leaves her clothes on the floor in the bedroom, and even her shoes are lined up perfectly in the bottom of the closet. So was it me?

Deena came back into the kitchen. "You ready to go to the jeweler's, Mace?" she asked in a real friendly voice.

We headed out the front door and up the block. The day was blazing hot. Even though it was still morning, the heat was pushing down on me, making it hard to stand up straight, to walk, to feel happy about anything. Ty carried the locket. I couldn't wait until it was gone.

The jeweler was on Frankford Avenue. A small display window at street level was filled with rings and sparkling necklaces, but the store itself was on the second floor over a clothing shop. We thudded up the narrow, carpeted staircase and opened the glass door. A wave of air conditioning flooded over us and it felt good, even if it did give me goose bumps.

The bell chimed when we entered and a tall man in a suit looked over at us. He was standing behind a short white swinging door in a separate little area, and he had a weird-looking magnifying glass strapped to his head. He didn't seem happy to see us. I think he was about to chase us away when Mrs. Quinn came out of the back room.

"Well, hello, Macey," she said.

Mrs. Quinn is on the PTO board at our school and she helps out in my class a lot whenever the teacher asks for volunteers. I don't think her son Liam likes it when she comes in, but the rest of us do. I wouldn't have minded if my mom came in. It would be bad only if you had a weird mother who wore strange clothes or acted goofy. Mrs. Quinn wasn't like that.

"What brings you into the store today?" She stood behind the glass display case and smiled at us. Necklaces and bracelets glittered under the lights.

"This is my sister, Deena, and my friend, Ty, and we found something. We wanted to ask you if it was valuable or not." I started to feel a little panicky. I didn't know if they charged for something like that and we didn't have much money on us.

"Here, let me see." Mrs. Quinn put out her long-fingered hand and Ty dropped the locket into it.

A little square of green velvet sat on top of the glass counter, and Mrs. Quinn carefully placed the locket on it and smoothed out the chain. "What a shame it's broken," she said. "It's so pretty. Let me show it to Tom."

She took the velvet square back behind the little white door and Tom stared down at it with his weird telescope eye. They talked quietly for a minute, then Mrs. Quinn flowed back out and behind the counter.

"Okay, girls," she began. "It's a nice locket but, of course, it's broken. It's not worth very much. The locket is fourteen-karat gold, but the chain is not. If you want to leave it here, we could try to see if we can find a place to order another half that will match. It might take a little while, though." Her nails were painted a deep pink that perfectly matched her lipstick. Her perfume smelled like hyacinths.

"Thank you, Mrs. Quinn," Deena answered in her politest voice, plucking the locket from the velvet square. "We need to think about it some more."

"Sure. That's fine. You girls enjoy the rest of your day."

Deena and Ty headed for the door, but Mrs. Quinn had put her hand on my arm. "How have you been, Macey? Are you doing okay?"

I'm not sure if all of the parents of my classmates know that Mom never came back, but Mrs. Quinn sure does. I can tell that she's only trying to be nice, but the way she's always asking me if I'm okay, with that worried look in her eyes, makes me feel like I have an incurable disease.

"I'm fine, thank you," I insisted. "Say hi to Liam for me." I added that last part to be polite. It's the kind of thing Dad would say.

"I will," she answered. "I'll see you again in September, but you can stop in here anytime you want."

Ty and Deena were waiting for me on the sidewalk.

"So it's not even worth anything," Deena mused.

"It's probably just the sentimental value," Ty added. "Why else could he possibly want it?"

"Maybe the numbers on it are a code or something," I guessed.

Deena rolled her eyes. "Macey, it's just two numbers. Even you could remember them."

It was mean, but it was true. Even I could remember two numbers, especially when they were Mom's birthday.

"Anyway," Deena continued, "people don't engrave codes in lockets. It doesn't make any sense."

I wanted to remind her that nothing about this whole thing made any sense. Something was wrong. We were missing something, but I couldn't figure it out. It was probably obvious, right there in front of our faces, and we couldn't see it.

"Are we going to go put it in the pipe now?" Ty asked.

"Yeah, we should," Deena said. "And then the whole thing will be over. Are you okay with that, Macey?"

I nodded. I was very okay with it. I wanted to be rid of the locket in the worst way. It seemed so simple. What could possibly go wrong? All we had to do was put the necklace in the pipe and it would be as if none of this had ever happened. At the time, I never could have imagined that the locket would come back to me again. I'll probably have it with me forever, a reminder of all the things that went wrong, of all the mistakes I made.

14

Sometimes I wonder about coincidences and how little things can change your whole life. Like what if my parents had gone to the adoption people a week earlier or a week later than they did? I could be living in a whole different city or even country. I might have a different religion and a different name. For Deena and Ty, everything was set the minute they were born—their parents, their family, their history. Sometimes I think of me lying behind glass with all the other babies, like the meats at the deli counter in a supermarket. Each time the buzzer goes off and the "number served" changes, a different couple steps forward with their little ticket and gets handed a baby. Almost like a game, a whole other life waited for me with each set of parents, all determined by a ticket, a place in line. Did I win? The question slipped into my head so fast that I couldn't stop it. I was suddenly ashamed. Of course I won. I couldn't imagine a life without Dad or Deena, and Mom was a good mother and she loved me as long as she was able.

Another coincidence I think of is, what would have happened if Deena and I had used our passes and taken the bus instead of walking to the deli? We never would have seen what was happening in front of Kevin's Discount Furniture Store. Of course, it would have been better for everyone if I had only slept late and never found the locket in the first place. Coincidences can drive you crazy. They never seem to end.

Frank's Deli, where we had to put the locket, was about ten blocks south on Frankford Avenue. It wouldn't have been such a terrible walk, except that it felt like it was getting ten degrees hotter by the minute. Those wavy lines were rising off the blacktopped streets and the cars looked as though they were riding toward small pools of simmering dark waters. Mom explained to me a bunch of times why those mirages formed, but I still can't remember. It's another one of those things that I couldn't seem to keep in my head and which disappointed her so much.

It was so hot that even Ty didn't feel like talking, and we trudged along the avenue like those plane-crash survivors who drag themselves across the desert. My missing thumb was aching again. I put my hand up to my chest and cradled it there while I walked. Sometimes that helps.

Frankford Avenue is lined with stores and nail salons and Chinese take-outs. All the grates were up by now, and I was getting jealous of the few shoppers wandering around in the air conditioning.

"Deena, let's go in the dollar store," I suggested. "It's on the next block and we can cool off a little."

"I'm thirsty," Ty said. "Let's go in the Hong Luck and beg for a soda."

"They're not going to give us free soda," I insisted.

"Well, they should," Ty countered. "My dad gets take-out there a lot. We're good customers. Hey, Deena, don't you think you should give free soda to good customers?"

Deena was fishing around inside her pocket and came up with a few crumpled bills and some change. "I have enough. We can buy some."

"Okay," Ty said, "but let me try begging first. It'll be fun."

The bell tinkled as we walked into the small shop. The smells of fried rice and spring rolls overwhelmed me and I was suddenly hungry as well as thirsty.

"Hey, Mrs. Lee." Ty waved into the back where steam was rising from boiling pots and frying pans were sizzling.

"Hello, Ty." Mrs. Lee wiped her hands on her apron and came, smiling, to the counter. "What can I get for you?"

"Well, it's like this. Me and my friends here, we got a long walk and we're dyin' of thirst. Then we saw your place and we thought maybe you would give us a little drink of water ... or maybe even soda ... so we don't get heatstroke or something on the way." Ty let her jaw drop and her tongue hang out of her mouth. I shrank a little toward the door. Deena seemed to be absorbed in the hem of her shirt.

"You want free drink? Hmmm ..." Mrs. Lee yelled something in Chinese to her husband, who was cooking in the back.

He answered her and shook his head, but a small smile cracked the edges of his tight-set mouth. I loved the sound of their conversation and wished that I could understand it all. Mrs. Chen taught me a few words and phrases and I can remember them just fine. You would think that if I could remember Chinese, I could remember why mirages form and how airplanes fly. But I can't.

"Tell you what." Mrs. Lee pulled a plastic bag out from under the counter. "You clean paper and trash from front of store, I give you soda. Deal?"

Ty laughed. "It's a deal."

Deena was disgusted, but I didn't mind. We picked up the stray newspapers, candy wrappers, and drink cups and stuffed them into the bag. It wasn't anything worse than what I did at home. I wouldn't touch the cigarette butts, though, and neither would Deena or Ty.

When we were coming out of the Hong Luck with our sodas, we saw Eugene. To be honest, the crowd attracted my attention first, and Ryan, who was sitting on his bike a little back from the rest. I wanted to explain to him why I had been out last night and not at home like I had promised. And that things weren't what they looked like, with Eugene's arm around my shoulder. Ryan had the wrong idea. When I got closer and heard Zach's voice, I knew something bad was happening to somebody. And that somebody turned out to be Eugene.

15

I feel shaky and upset whenever I see somebody getting picked on for no good reason, especially when he's bleeding and so outnumbered like Eugene was. I know why those kids did it, though. Eugene was different, he was new, and he was really, really fat. He was the perfect target, at least in our neighborhood. Zach would never have been brave enough if Eugene had been tall or athletic or in any way cool.

In our house, Deena and I are never permitted to say anything bad about anyone. We can't complain at the dinner table, like other kids do, about how our partner in a school project was a dork or smelled bad or was foreign. We're not allowed to make any general comments about anybody's race or physical appearance.

I'm sure that's a good thing, especially since we don't really know what my race is. Maybe I'm good at remembering Chinese phrases because I am part Chinese. But maybe I'm Hispanic. I think I have African American hair, but so does Ariele and she's Jewish. The bad thing about not knowing is that you don't really have a group to belong to and feel a part of. The Russian kids always sit together at lunch, and the Koreans have their own special church. The Chinese have cool traditions and celebrations, and even the Liberians, like Ty's family, have a club that they belong to. Dad is proud of being Irish and I suppose that I'm adopted Irish, but it isn't the same. I don't look like any Irish person I've ever met, not even my own family, and I hate corned beef and cabbage. Deena says that it doesn't matter, that we're all Americans, and she could care less what her nationality is. I think, though, that it's easier to not care when you already know. Sometimes I'd just like to know.

There is one good thing about not knowing, though. When different groups don't get along, I never have to be for one side or the other. I can stay out of it. But that day, I couldn't stay out of it. Not when I saw what was happening to Eugene. It wasn't right. I'm sure he didn't do anything to them, and they didn't even know him.

About ten kids were bunched in front of Kevin's Discount Furniture Store, mostly guys, and some of them were laughing so hard that they were holding their stomachs. I walked up to the edge of the circle to see what was going on and peered past Joe's shoulder. My heart did a huge thump when I saw Eugene flailing on the ground, helpless as a beached whale. Blood covered his knee and was running down his leg and staining his sock. An old greenish suitcase was broken open on the sidewalk and all the contents were spilled out. Eugene's T-shirts and shorts and combs and Mitchum deodorant stick were strewn across the concrete. He was frantically trying to collect some of his photos with one hand while he protected the others against his chest.

"Oooohhhh, look at me. Aren't I pretty?" Zach held up a

pair of Eugene's giant boxer shorts. "It's a dress!" he exclaimed. "Or ... or ..." He held the boxers over his head. "It could be the sail to a really big ship."

"Maybe it's a tablecloth!" Joe yelled.

"Or the tarp they use to cover the baseball field when it rains," called Dmitri.

I shot a look at Ryan, but he only smirked and then stared down at his handlebars. He was mad at me. I pushed past Joe and ripped the boxers out of Zach's hand. I don't know what I was thinking, or even if I was thinking, when I went after Zach. I thumped him hard in the chest with my left hand, my fingers curled into a fist.

"Ooooooooh," the kids murmured after I struck the blow.

Zach wasn't expecting it and he lost his balance, falling backward over a shampoo bottle and hitting the ground hard. I was so angry I couldn't even speak. I stood over him, panting hard.

But it took Zach only a second to jump to his feet.

"Don't touch me, Niner!" he screamed. "What do you think you're doing?" His face was red and his eyes wild. "Are you trying to save your fat booooooyfriend?" He was frantically brushing off the front of his shirt, like I had infected him with germs or bugs. He pointed at me but looked at the guys standing around us. "She touched me with her slimy, deformed, gross hand! You all saw it. What do you think of that? What should I do about it, huh?"

Zach was playing to the crowd now, not looking at me, but I noticed him slowly moving closer to where I stood. He must have thought I was stupid, but I'm not. I was ready. He lunged at me, arms outstretched, but I was quicker and darted out of the way. I jumped over the suitcase and around Eugene. The circle of kids widened and quieted down. I could almost hear them licking their lips in anticipation. I had no chance of winning. I never fought. And Zach was bigger and stronger. They were all waiting to watch him bash my face in. Some of them were my friends.

My only advantage was my speed and I didn't know how much it would help me in that small circle. The sun was baking the top of my head, and I could feel the heat rising off the sidewalk as Zach and I did our little dance around the perimeter of the circle.

"Getting nervous, Niner?" He moved to the left and so did I, keeping the maximum distance between us. "I missed on purpose the first time, you little freak."

Sweat was leaking from my armpits and rolling down my sides, and my tongue was stuck to the roof of my mouth. Someone in the circle gave me a shove in the back, and I stumbled toward Zach for a second before scuttling back into my position. A ripple of laughter went around the circle. I was still clutching the full cup of Coke from the Hong Luck. I must have been gripping it too hard because I felt cold soda running over my hand. But I didn't take my eyes off Zach.

"You're going to die, Niner." The laughter seemed to have pumped him up. "How does it feel, freak?"

And all of a sudden, I could see how much Zach was enjoying himself. He had probably been looking forward to a moment like this for a long time. Hadn't he wanted to hit me during the kickball game and when I beat him at school in the 100-meter trials? And how many other times had he screamed in my face, his fists clenched? A sheen of sweat was gleaming on his face now, but he was smiling. Deena was yelling something in the background, but I couldn't hear what it was. I was too focused on Zach.

When the first swing came, I ducked and spun away from him. He followed with another quick right, but again I was quicker. I couldn't dodge him forever and his anger was back as quick as it had left. He wasn't missing on purpose, and the kids knew it. They let out low sounds of admiration, *ooohs* and *aaaaahs*, and some laughed. Zach wouldn't be happy until they all saw him get me good. I thought about attacking him instead of dodging the blows, but I didn't want to hit him. I didn't want to be anywhere near him. I watched his eyes. He lunged at me again and in desperation I chucked my soda at him. It was a bull's-eye. The lid came off and I got him smack in the face with twelve ounces of Coke and ice. He sputtered and dripped and coughed. But only for a second. The kids were screaming with laughter, but Zach turned scary and wild, howling and charging at me like a wounded lion. I tried to squeeze out of the circle, but Joe pushed me back in. There was nowhere to go. At the last second and with per- fect timing, Eugene, who had been sitting as still as a rock, stuck out his leg. Zach tripped over it and went flying, but I wasn't far enough out of the way and he grabbed me on the way down. We both tumbled hard to the sidewalk. Zach was frantic and still howling, and before I could move, he pinned my arm to the cement and punched my right shoulder. I tried to twist away, but he had me tight. He raised up his fist to whack me in the face.

I was about to turn my head away from the blow when I saw Ryan jump in and grab his brother's wrist in midair. "C'mon, Zach. Knock it off. You don't want to fight a girl." Ryan was shaking his head. I couldn't tell if he was more disgusted with me or with Zach. I wanted to catch his eye for a second so he would know how I felt, how glad I was that he was there, how bad I felt about last night. But Ryan wouldn't look at me at all. I tried to say his name, but my throat was all choked up. I swallowed down the lump and narrowed my eyes. I won and Zach is nothing but a loser, I thought. I tried not to think about Ryan at all. I tried not to feel how much it hurt that he wouldn't even look at me. I lay very still against the hot cement. I felt it burning into the back of my skull and I concentrated on that feeling and tried to ignore everything else.

Zach was spitting curse words at me, some that I had never even heard before. He screamed that I wasn't a girl anyway, that I was a deformed "thing," and he called me all kinds of names. His hair was plastered to the side of his head from the sweat and the soda. He was still trying to hit me, but Ryan had wrapped him in a bear hug and was pulling him away. I was never so glad that Ryan was the bigger, stronger twin. Zach managed to swing his leg once he was up off the ground and he caught me good in my left shoulder with a hard kick.

When Ryan and Zach were gone, the crowd of kids started

to filter away. The ones who were my friends most of the time stopped and asked me if I was okay.

"Good job, Mace," Carlos said. "You handled him, all right. That Zach is some kind of psycho."

And then they were all gone, and Eugene and I were left lying on the sidewalk surrounded by his toothpaste and dental floss and sour-smelling clothes. My shoulders were throbbing and my left elbow was bleeding from the fall. I closed my eyes and wished I could melt into the cracks in the cement like an abandoned Popsicle. I'd like to say that I was brave, that I got up and dusted myself off and shouted a few of my own curses after Zach and those other kids. But I wasn't brave. I lay on the sidewalk and let myself cry, the tears silently rolling down my face and trickling into my ears. And if I had to say what I was crying about, I couldn't even do it. All I knew was that I wasn't crying about Zach or anything he did. I felt like I was melting.

Deena dropped down beside me. "Oh, my God, Macey, what were you thinking? Are you okay? Here, let me help you sit up."

"I'm okay." I winced, a soreness catching in my shoulder. "He makes me so mad."

"We tried to help you," Ty insisted. "But they wouldn't let us. Dylan and Carlos were holding me back, squeezing my arms, and Javier had a hold of Deena."

"I kicked him as hard as I could in the shins," Deena boasted. "I don't know who he thinks he is. I didn't even think he liked Zach."

"He probably just likes fights," I said, quickly wiping my

eyes. Any one of those kids could have stopped Zach, but they all wanted to watch what would happen. And I couldn't exactly complain. How many times had I stood in the crowd in the school yard and watched a fight without ever doing anything to stop it?

"Are you okay, Eugene?" I asked.

Eugene was busy putting all his stuff back in the suitcase, but the clasp was clearly busted. It wouldn't stay shut. He didn't answer me.

"You goin' somewhere?" Ty asked.

"Yeah, how come you've got a suitcase anyway?" Deena tried to help him close the clasp, but he pushed her hand away.

"Okay, fine," Deena spat. "See what you get when you try to help somebody, Macey? I don't know why you stuck up for him in the first place. Let's get out of here."

Eugene had turned toward the brick wall of the furniture store and continued to fiddle with the suitcase. I watched his shoulders, though. They were drooped more than ever and they were shaking. Eugene wasn't okay.

"Could you guys go back in the Hong Luck and ask Mrs. Lee for a cup of water and some napkins?" I pointed to my bloody elbow. "I don't want to go around like this."

"Just come with us," Deena ordered. "She'll let you use the bathroom in the back. Your face is all smeary, too, you know."

"No. I'm not going in there. She'll ask me a thousand questions and I'll have to lie and everything and say nothing happened. Please?"

"Oh, all right." Deena marched off.

"Ty?" I called. "Can you get some string, too?" I pointed to Eugene's suitcase and made a tying motion with my hands.

Ty nodded. "Got it."

Eugene wouldn't talk to me even after they were gone.

"Eugene," I said, "I'm real sorry about today at my house. I don't know why I got mad and all. You didn't do anything. I messed everything up. And I'm sorry about those kids, too. They're jerks."

He sat with his back to me and fingered the sides of his suitcase.

"Okay," I continued. "I'm a jerk, too. I admit it."

He didn't respond.

"C'mon, Eugene. Please don't be mad at me. At least say something."

He fiddled with the suitcase some more. "I'm not mad at you," he finally sighed. And then, without saying another word, he stood and limped into the alley behind the store, dragging his suitcase along the ground.

I sat on the hot, dirty sidewalk and watched him disappear into the gloomy shadows between the two stores. He was mad. I ran my finger down the line of sticky blood on my arm. Tears had dried on my cheeks and the skin felt tight all around them. I leaned back against the building and watched the traffic on Frankford Avenue, scanning the faces in all the cars, like usual. But even if she was there somewhere, my birth mother, the one who was in my blood, whose genes I had, she didn't want me anyway. I had to face it. I turned and looked at my reflection in the display window. I didn't want to be alone. I got up and followed Eugene. He was sitting on a step leading to the service entrance at the rear of the furniture store, repacking his suitcase.

"I just want to be by myself," he said without looking up. "Can you please go away?"

"But where are you going to go?" I asked.

"I'm going to find my aunt."

Eugene was carefully and meticulously folding his clothes. I sat next to him on the step and watched in silence.

"I could help," I finally said. "Deena and Ty could, too. We could use the phone book, and Deena and me have passes for the bus because our dad works at fixing them. So we could get around easier. Eugene, let me tell them."

"Tell us what?" Ty asked. She and Deena popped their heads around the corner.

"What are you trying to do, hide from us?" Deena complained. "Didn't you hear me calling you?"

"Sorry," I said. "I didn't want to hang out on the sidewalk anymore."

Ty slipped me the string and I threaded it through the handle and around Eugene's suitcase. He just sat with his head in his hands. I tried to knot the string, but I was having some trouble. It's hard when you're missing a thumb. Ty leaned over to help. She gave me a look. The suitcase smelled really bad, like it had been stewing in a vat of sweat and mold. Eugene didn't have a suitcase last night, and I knew he didn't have a house to keep it in. He must have stashed it somewhere outside and it got soaked in the storm.

I took one of the cups of water and a wad of napkins and washed off my arm. Then I started on my face.

"Are you going somewhere, Eugene?" Deena asked. "How come you got a suitcase?"

Eugene was still breathing hard and his face was all gray. I picked up the second cup of water and handed it to him. "Drink this," I said. I thought his stomach needed it more than his knee. I wish I had known back then what he really needed, but even he didn't know. His mother should have known, though, and right after myself, I blame her.

16

Eugene had money and so we all ended up going back to the Hong Luck and ordering lunch. We ate lo mein at the small plastic table that was squeezed between the counter and the front window. Eugene barely fit in the chair. His money had been stolen from his stepdad, and maybe that meant that I was eating stolen food. I didn't know if a person could get arrested for that. But that wasn't the thing that was affecting my appetite. I twirled the noodles around with my chopsticks, but I couldn't put any of them in my mouth.

"Did you *see* his face when you hit him with that soda?" Deena laughed.

"It was awesome. He looked like this." Ty twisted her mouth and squinted her eyes. "*Ppppht, ppppht, ppppht.*"

"What's that supposed to be?" I asked.

"That's Zach, spitting '*ppppht, ppppht*' after you hit him. It was so good! I wish I could watch it on instant replay." Ty suddenly stopped laughing. "You know what, though, Macey? He's going to get you back sooner or later. He's a weird dude and he holds a grudge. You gotta be careful."

"I'm not worried about him," I said. And I wasn't really.

Zach is mostly a coward. He would call me a lot of names next week and try to trip me and knock me on the ground or something. But he wouldn't hide in the alley and stab me or anything like that. He is Ryan's twin, after all. But it made me wonder. If I was all beat-up and lying in a hospital bed with tubes coming out of me everywhere, would Mom come back to see me? Maybe I wouldn't want her back. I tried to picture it. I imagined her pushing open the swinging hospital-room door, seeing Deena right away. She'd throw her arms around her, asking her about school and report cards and the Mathletes competitions. Then she'd turn to me in the bed and shake her head with a "tsk-tsk," thinking to herself, "What has Macey done to herself now?" And Dad, he'd be glad to see her, too. And maybe the three of them would go out to dinner, to catch up. I'd have to convince Dad to go without me, but I'd make him go. And I wouldn't be mad at him or Deena. I know they would come back for me.

"Ty's right, Macey," Deena said. "And you, too, Eugene. We should walk you home or something."

"It's too far." He said it into his plate, real low, like he was talking only to himself, but I heard him.

"What?" Ty asked.

"He said that it's too far." I answered for Eugene. He had eaten even less of his lunch than I had. That should have been a very big clue, but I missed it.

"Well, duh," Deena said. "I don't mean your *home* home, I mean where you're staying here with your aunt. Wasn't it your aunt?"

Eugene pushed his noodles from one side of his plate to the other. Little waves of brown soy sauce lapped at the edges.

"Eugene." I tried to get him to look up at me, but he wouldn't. "Deena and Ty won't tell. They're good at keeping secrets."

"What? What secret?" Deena asked.

Eugene stared at Deena. "I ran away, okay? Are you happy?"

Deena and Ty sat frozen with their forks in midair, their mouths open. Neither one said anything.

Deena finally leaned forward across the small table and dropped her voice to a whisper. "You ran away all the way from Florida to Philadelphia?"

Eugene nodded.

Ty whistled. "Wow."

"Why?" Deena asked. "What happened?"

Eugene drew his finger through the condensation on his soft-drink cup. He didn't answer.

Deena stared at Eugene's battered suitcase. The yellowed sleeve of a T-shirt was sticking out the side. It was speckled with dirt from the sidewalk.

"So you're not really staying with your aunt or anybody, are you?" she asked.

Eugene shook his head.

"But where do you sleep?"

He shrugged. "I slept at your house last night."

Deena looked at me.

"He's actually got an aunt in Philadelphia," I said, "but we've got to help him find her."

"But where'd you sleep before last night?" Deena pressed.

She was leaning closer to Eugene with each question and looked almost like she was ready to stick her hand down his throat and pull out the answers she was looking for. Deena's never satisfied until she has all the facts and can add everything up and get the perfect solution, like one of her math problems. Sometimes I wonder if that's why she's always been so mad at Mom. She took some important facts with her when she left us, and so Deena can't figure out what happened. There is no exact solution to the problem of our missing mother. It just hangs out there open and unfinished. Dad says that life doesn't always work out neatly like you think it should. I've always known that, of course, because my life never did add up perfectly. I'm missing the first two parts of the equation: birth mother plus birth father equals me. I wonder if Dad knows who they are. We've never talked about it. I wonder if it would hurt his feelings if I asked him.

Eugene was stabbing his egg roll with a toothpick. "I slept on the bus. I just got here yesterday."

"Well, don't you know where your aunt lives?" Deena was practically on her feet and I tugged her shirt until she fell back into her chair.

A customer came into the shop and we all pretended to be interested in our food until he paid for his order and left.

Eugene pushed his plate away. "She moved."

"Check your fortune cookie, Eugene," Ty said. "They have lucky numbers in there. They could be, like, clues to your aunt's new address."

"Ty, you've been watching too many movies," I said. "We need a better plan than that."

Deena snatched the cookie in front of Eugene. She popped it open and read the fortune.

"What's it say?" Ty asked.

"Nothing. It's stupid." Deena crumpled the little slip of paper and threw it in the trash. She never did tell us what Eugene's fortune was, even afterward, when everything was over. I don't believe in fortunes anyway. And besides, I'm sure that no cookie could have predicted what was about to happen to us.

We finally decided that the first thing we had to do was take the locket to the deli and stick it in the pipe. Then we could forget about that whole thing and concentrate on finding Eugene's aunt. We would start by asking at neighbors' houses and checking the local stores to see if anyone knew her. If that didn't work, we could search for her online and in the phone book. Deena seemed way more excited about it than Eugene did.

Deena suggested that we stop at Grandma's house on the way so that we could store Eugene's suitcase someplace safe. We could sneak it in the back door to Deena and Grandma would never know. Deena had a good idea, but she was going to have to do it alone.

Ty, Eugene, and I sat by the cellar door and waited for her. At least we had shade here, and the stone walls were cool. I felt shaky at first, thinking of the creepy guy who pinned me against the door in this very spot, but it seemed so different today. The sun was out, ladies were hanging wash up and down the alley, and kids were playing on their bikes and in their little pools.

Eugene sat with his back against one wall, and Ty and I leaned against the other. The space was so small we had to keep our knees bent to keep from kicking each other.

Eugene had a small stone and he was scraping it against a crack in the cement between his feet. As I watched him, I got another one of those bad feelings. Worry was curling around inside my stomach, but I didn't know why. Eugene was working so hard with his stone, like he was trying to unearth a fossil. He suddenly stopped and looked up at me. "How come your grandmother doesn't like you, Macey?"

My mouth dropped open. I thought for a minute, not sure if Eugene was being rude by asking me such a thing. But it is something I've wondered about a lot. Grandma's not like regular people, though. She's kind of different. I would be more upset if the Chens didn't like me or Ty's parents or Mrs. Fitz. Then I would wonder what was wrong with me. But with Grandma, it seems normal. It's like the stain on the ceiling above my bed. I don't like it, but it's been there so long that it's just a regular part of the room and I don't lose any sleep over it.

Eugene stopped his scraping for a minute and he and Ty were staring at me, waiting.

I shrugged at them. "I don't know why she doesn't like me. It doesn't really matter."

"Yes it does," Ty said. "How could she not like you?"

"Well, I'm not sure if this is the reason, but I remember one time when I was about eight or nine years old, I broke one of her favorite plates. Her mother had given it to her when she got married and it was really old and valuable and I smashed it to pieces. And she said ..." I stopped, too embarrassed to go on.

"What?" Ty asked. "She said what?"

"Nothing."

"C'mon," Ty urged. "You can tell us."

"What did she say?" Eugene pressed.

"It's nothing really. She just said ..." The memory came flooding back and I could feel my face burning. "She said that it just showed how I wasn't her real granddaughter."

"You're her granddaughter and you're real," Eugene said. "So what was she talking about?"

"You know what I mean. I'm adopted. I'm not her real granddaughter."

"That's stupid," Ty said.

"It's totally stupid," Eugene agreed.

"No. It makes sense." I started to defend Grandma because she may have actually been right that time. I didn't care about that stupid plate. Deena loved it. It was an antique or something and it had these green partridges and yellow pears all over it. Whenever we went to dinner at Grandma's, Deena always got to eat from that plate. Even now I'm not sure if I didn't drop it on purpose. It had been passed down for generations in our family, and maybe if I was real, the way Deena was real, it would have meant something to me and I would have taken better care of it. But to me it was just a horrible old plate and I was secretly glad that it was broken. The mean, ugly part of me that I hide from everyone was happy for the rest of that day and every time afterward that we ate at Grandma's.

"It doesn't make sense!" Ty was getting mad. "Don't say that. Do your dad and mom not like you because you're adopted and Deena isn't?"

I shook my head. My parents loved me just as much as they loved Deena. I disappointed Mom with my bad grades and my messy room, but plenty of kids do that. Mom loved me. I know she did, even if sometimes it felt like Deena was her favorite.

"I know why your grandmother doesn't like you." Ty pinched the skin on my forearm. "It's because of this."

"What do you mean?"

"'Cause you're black."

"Really? You think I'm black?" Ty and I had never discussed our race before. It just didn't matter.

"Well, you ain't white. Put your arms out," she ordered.

Eugene, Ty, and I lined up our arms. Ty is a dark chocolate, Eugene a pasty white, and I am somewhere in between.

"She could be both white and black," Eugene said. "Maybe you're half-and-half."

"Maybe." I ran my finger up and down my arm. "I could be Hispanic or Arab or Chinese, too."

"Chinese!?" Ty laughed and slapped my arm. "You don't look anything like a Chinese person."

"She could be." Eugene stuck up for me. "I'm like ten different things. I can't even remember them all. Polish and Irish and English. I think Swedish, too. My dad was part Swedish."

"Yeah, but I bet you're not Chinese," Ty said.

Eugene laughed. "No, I don't think I'm Chinese. But you never know. I knew this kid in school and his father was Iranian, but the kid had real white skin and red hair like his mom. Not a bit of the Iranian showed in him. I could be part Chinese and it just doesn't show."

"I doubt it," Ty said. "I bet you a million dollars that you are not part Chinese. You ask your mom and dad, and when you find out I'm right, you have to send me a million dollars."

Eugene went back to digging his stone into the crack in the cement.

I gave Ty a look.

"Oh, sorry, Eugene," she gushed. "I totally forgot for a minute that you ran away. But you'll go back sooner or later, right?"

Ty wasn't being insensitive or anything. She just can't imagine anybody wanting to live away from their family. She has a great mother and father, an older brother who is always looking out for her, and a cute little sister who adores her. From the start, Ty has been convinced that my mother will come home, too. Our house is like Ty's second home and our family like an extension of her own. It makes no sense to her that my mother would stay away.

"I am *never* going back." Eugene shoved the stone so hard into the crack that he scraped his finger against the cement and it began to bleed.

"But why not?" Ty asked. "Why did you run away in the first place?"

We heard the ten thousand bolts sliding back, and Deena slowly opened the basement door so that it wouldn't creak too loudly. She put her finger to her lips, then motioned for the suitcase. We passed it to her and she slid it inside. "I'll be out in a minute," she whispered. "Meet me out front."

Eugene was the first one up and out into the alley. He didn't answer the question and Ty didn't ask it again. We had to get the necklace into the pipe behind the deli and that was what we talked about all the way there. But Eugene was mostly quiet and dragging behind us, and I was mostly thinking about him. I glanced back at him a bunch of times. Sweat rolled down the sides of his face and his wet T-shirt clung to his distended stomach. I asked him if he was okay, but he waved me away with a flick of his hand. Finding Eugene's aunt was going to be like a game for Deena and Ty and me, something different and fun to do on a hot summer day. But it meant a whole lot more to Eugene. I couldn't even imagine what it felt like to be him, a stranger, totally alone in a new city.

I wish that we had looked for Eugene's aunt first and taken the necklace to the deli later. Then maybe he would have had a good home, even if it was only for a little while. Instead, it was the police who found Eugene's aunt. And the necklace that started all the trouble is still in my pocket.

17

We thought we had everything figured out. After we put the necklace in the pipe, we would start our search for Eugene's aunt. If we didn't find her on the first day, we would sneak Eugene into Grandma's basement and he could sleep on an old cot that was down there. Dad would get too suspicious if Eugene kept sleeping over at our house and, even though Deena and I knew Dad would help, Eugene made us swear about ten times that we would keep his secret. Grandma can't do steps, so she would never know that he was in the basement. Even Eugene liked the plan and he perked up a little bit when we got to the deli on Frankford Avenue. We thought we were so smart. It was almost like we were in some exciting TV show, solving a big mystery. But it didn't turn out like TV. The bad guys didn't get caught and all the problems weren't solved at the end of the hour.

Frankford Avenue is lined with shops and storefront churches and hair salons. Some of the places are boarded up, but most of them are still open. The avenue runs in a straight line for miles, through lots of neighborhoods. In our neighborhood, though, the elevated train runs directly over the street, and we've all gotten used to pausing in our conversations when a train squeals by overhead. It's just a part of being on the avenue. Even in the stores, there's a rhythm to the squeal of the el. The salesman pauses with the product in his hand and the customer stares at the shelf. The nail-salon owner holds her brush in the air and steadies the bottle with her hand. In less than a minute, the train clacks away and everybody goes on with what they were doing. You can always tell an outsider by the way he or she cringes and looks up at the awful noise in surprise.

The deli was in the middle of the block. We had to go around the back to find the pipe. Behind each block of storefronts are two streets of row houses. The alley between the houses and the alley behind the stores form a T. It wasn't so easy to figure out which door in the back belonged to the deli. They all looked the same and there were no signs. I ran around to the front again and counted stores.

"Well," Deena asked when I came back, "which one is it?"

"This is the beauty school," I said as I walked. "Then comes the pretzel-factory store, the check-cashing place, and then the deli." I stopped in front of a blue door. "This has to be the deli. Anybody see a pipe?"

The backs of the stores were brick and they were grimy from years of exhaust and pollution. The cement on the ground was stained a permanent black from dirt, trash, and grease spills. There was a line of Dumpsters that smelled awful, stewing in the heat, and the alley was filled with flies. I wanted to find that pipe fast and get out of there.

"There!" Ty pointed up to a white plastic pipe that jutted out of the brick.

"That can't be it," I complained. "It's too high. How are we supposed to get up there?"

Ty jumped up and slapped the wall, and she was still a couple of feet short. Eugene linked his hands and boosted me up as high as he could go, but I couldn't reach it either.

"Well, there's no other pipe that I can see," Deena said. "Are you sure that this is the right place?"

"He said 'Frank's Deli.' This is the only Frank's Deli that I know of."

"We have to find something to stand on," Eugene suggested.

"Okay, this is totally gross," I said. "But I'll climb on top of the Dumpster and ..."

"It's too far from the pipe," Deena cut in.

"I know. But if Ty stands between the Dumpster and the pipe, and I can put one foot on her shoulder and one on the Dumpster, I think I can reach it."

"That's crazy." Deena shook her head. "You'll kill yourself."

"It's not like it's ten stories high, Deena. I'm not going to kill myself. Besides, do you have any other ideas?"

"Yeah, shorty," Ty teased. "Do you have any other ideas?"

Eugene gave me a leg up and I made it onto the Dumpster. The rotten smell filled my head and stomach and I had to swallow a few times to keep from throwing up. One side of it was open and it needed to be emptied real bad. Half-eaten sandwiches and paper cups and moldy meats were all festering down there. The metal of the Dumpster was hot and I could feel it burning through the soles of my sneakers.

I balanced on the edge and put my right hand against the brick to steady myself.

"Okay, Ty, I'm ready."

"Be careful, Macey," Deena warned.

Ty stood one long step away and I stretched out and put my left foot on her right shoulder. I leaned toward the pipe. My back was to the alley. When Deena screamed, I thought she was worried I would fall.

"I got it!" I yelled triumphantly. "Watch this!" I put both hands around the pipe and swung my feet to the wall. I clung there, kind of like Spider-Man, so proud of myself.

"Macey!" Deena screamed at me.

"What?" I screamed back, annoyed. But the odd tone in her voice made me look. Two men stood there. One held the back of Deena's shirt. One had Ty around the wrist.

Eugene looked up at me and then took off without a word.

"Get back here, kid!" one guy yelled.

"Let him go," said the other. "This'll only take a minute. Macey, is that your name?"

I watched Eugene disappear down the alley. He was running, swaying side to side as his weight shifted. He paused once to glance back at us, then disappeared around the corner. I looked at the guy who held my sister.

"Come down," he said. "C'mon, we're not going to hurt ya' if you hurry up. Let's go."

I gripped the pipe even tighter. Ty and Deena were absolutely still, their eyes huge. Everybody was staring at me. My throat had closed up, and I just stared back at them.

"I said, come down. Right now. I'm getting real tired of waiting."

I walked my feet up the wall a little bit but said nothing.

"Look, kid. I'm not a patient kind of guy, got it? I get really mad when I have to wait."

I dug the toes of my sneakers into a gap between the bricks. Some mortar came loose and crumbled to the ground. My mouth was dry as sand.

The guy began cursing at me and he shook Deena in his anger. I saw tears well up in her eyes. "Go get me something to poke her down with," he said to his friend.

"No. We don't have to bother. She's not going to last long up there," the dark-haired one said. "It'll only take another minute or two."

He was right. My arms were aching. I didn't know how much longer I could hold on.

"Yeah, well, we don't have a whole lot of time to fool around." He glanced over his shoulder.

I was looking up and down the alley now, too. Where were the kids on their bikes? Why didn't somebody come out to take in their laundry? It was dead quiet except for the hum of window air-conditioners and the buzz of the flies.

A car turned into the alley. A white-haired lady was driving with a bag of groceries on the seat beside her. A small black dog sat in her lap.

"Help!" I screamed at her. "Help! Call the police!" But her windows were up.

She drove right on by. I had shouted as loud as I could, but the el was clacking over the roof of the building. Its squeals had swallowed every word. My hands were wet with sweat and slipping. Fire shot through the muscles of my arms. There was no one left to call to.

The man holding Deena opened the palm of his hand and flashed a knife. "Get down now," he ordered. "Or else."

Deena began to cry. I let go and fell hard to the ground.

I was sprawled on the cement, old straws, cigarette butts, and crumpled wrappers around me. He crouched down next to me, dragging Deena with him. "Give it to me," he demanded. His breath was sour and smoky.

I dropped the necklace into his outstretched hand. I was glad to get rid of it.

He stared hard at me for a second, mouth open, and then his face twisted in anger. He was a white man, but a blackness seemed to spread under his eyes. "You think you're funny?" he screamed, his spit sprinkling my face. I turned away. He threw the necklace at me. "Do you? This isn't some kind of game!"

I shook my head. "I know. But I thought … I thought …"

"Where's the money?" He shoved me hard in the chest and my head banged up against the wall.

"Wha' … what money?" I mumbled, trying to scramble away from him.

Deena was sobbing now.

"Don't fool with me, kid. You see this?" He flashed the knife again. "I'll use it if you don't tell me where the money is. We know you took it. It's not yours. Did you put it in the pipe?"

I had no idea what money he was talking about. I thought about Eugene and the money he stole. But if that was what they were after, why didn't they chase Eugene?

"She didn't put it in the pipe. I'd've seen it," the other guy said. "Maybe she dropped it in the Dumpster."

"Did you drop it in the Dumpster, huh?" He prodded my shoulder with the dull end of the switchblade.

"I swear I don't know what you're talking about. Please. Leave us alone."

He stared up at the sky, his jaw jutting sharply from his face. Dark stubble ran up his neck and over a tattoo of a snake. He had a tic under his left eye and his cheek was pulsing with it. I felt around in the gunk behind me for a bottle or a piece of glass or anything I could use. But then it dawned on me that he couldn't hold onto Deena, the knife, and me all at the same time. So I jumped up from the ground. "HELP!" I yelled. "Somebody HELP us!"

He let go of Deena and roughly clamped his hand over my mouth, pushing my head back against the brick wall. But she didn't run. She just stood there crying. I didn't know if she was too scared to move or if she didn't want to leave me.

"Run, Deena, run!" I tried to say through his thick fingers. I struggled to get free of him.

The back door of the deli swung open and slammed against the wall. A bearded man in a white apron stood in the doorway and looked down at us.

The guy holding me started back, pointing his knife in every direction. I flattened myself against the brick. Another el was squealing down the tracks, and we all stood as though frozen by its sound. As it moved away, I could clearly hear the sound of an approaching siren. The two men took off, running out of the alley toward Wellington Street.

"What's going on?" the deli man asked. "Are you kids okay?"

I didn't stop to answer. I grabbed Deena's arm, and she and Ty and I ran, too, in the opposite direction that the men had gone.

"Hey! Come back!" the deli man called.

But we didn't. We ran until our chests heaved and our throats burned. We ran across streets, between cars and shoppers, ignoring red lights and stop signs. I tried to think only of my feet slapping the hot cement, but I could still smell him, still feel his oily fingers on my face. Sweat was pouring down my neck and back. Deena was gagging and wheezing behind me. I could almost hear her lungs filling up with phlegm.

"Slow down now, we can walk," I panted.

But she shook her head and kept going.

"Deena," I called. "Stop!"

If she didn't have asthma, I think she would have run all the way to Florida and into the ocean. When her legs started to shake and give out, I linked her arm in mine and pulled her my way. Ty grabbed Deena's other arm and we steered her into the dollar store. I plopped Deena into one of the cheap plastic chairs that were on sale. She was crying.

An Indian woman in a blue pinafore came out from behind the counter. "You okay?" she asked. "What's wrong?"

"She's okay," I lied. "She has a problem with asthma and the heat is bothering her. Can she sit here in the air conditioning until she can breathe?"

"Yes, yes. Certainly, certainly. Sit."

"I'm sorry," Deena choked. "It's all my fault. We should've told Dad. I didn't think ... I didn't know. ..."

The Indian woman handed me a bottle of water. "Here. Give her this," she said. She leaned over Deena in a motherly way, her jewelry jangling, and patted her on the head. Deena shrank from the touch.

"Thank you for the water, ma'am." I unscrewed the top and handed the bottle to Deena. "Don't talk," I said. "Nothing is your fault."

She kept her mouth shut like I ordered, but she kept nodding and pointing to her chest. I pounded my hands up and down her back to loosen the phlegm.

Ty finally found her voice. "It's not your fault, Deena. We all agreed to do it." It wasn't until she spoke that I realized she hadn't said a word since I stood on her shoulder in the alley.

The tears silently dripped down Deena's face, but her breathing was becoming more relaxed.

"I can call a doctor for you," the storekeeper offered. "Or do you want to phone your mommy?"

The question hit Deena like a jolt of electricity. She went rigid in her chair. She tried to say something but was overcome with a spasm of coughing and doubled over in the seat.

"No, no, thank you," I answered. "She's fine now. Thank you so much for the water." I grabbed Deena and hustled her out of the store, still coughing. I would have liked to have stayed a little longer, until she had calmed down more, but we were creating too much of a scene in the store.

We dragged ourselves up Frankford Avenue toward home. Ty looked over her shoulder every five seconds and we avoided alleys.

"What if … they know … where we … live?" Deena wheezed.

Ty and I looked at each other. We slowed down. Deena was right. We couldn't go home. I hated the very thought, but we had to go to Grandma's. Deena had a spare inhaler there and, as long as we weren't being followed, we'd be safe.

I tried to sound cheerful about it. "We'll go to Grandma's and hang out in the air conditioning until Dad gets home."

Ty groaned. "No way. Let's go to my house."

"We can't," I said. "You live right behind us. If they're there, they'd see us go in and then they'd know where you live, too." Besides, I couldn't go to Ty's house. Her mother is one of those people I can't hide anything from. She looks right into me somehow. Whenever I go over, she always opens up her arms and folds me into her chest. She smells like spice and flowers, which is nice, but she holds me there sometimes until I can hardly breathe. She feeds me her special bread at the kitchen table and talks while she's working. She could make me confess to a murder I never committed. If I went over to Ty's, I would fall apart right away and I couldn't let myself do that. I had to see Dad. I had to explain things to him first.

"Don't worry, Ty. We can spend a lot of time in the basement. We'll say that we're doing the wash. We have to set up the cot for Eugene anyway."

"Yeah, where do you think Eugene is?" Ty asked.

"I don't know. Maybe he went to look for his aunt without us."

"Man, he ran a lot faster than I ever thought he could. That boy was moving."

"What ... money ... were they talking ... about ... those guys?" Deena puffed.

"I have no idea. Why would they think we had their money?" I reached into my pocket and pulled out the necklace. I stared down at the broken locket. I couldn't figure it out.

"I don't know what is going on," Ty said. "But we can't mess around with this anymore. You gotta tell your dad."

Deena was crying again. She was worrying me. "We'll be locked ... in the ... house ... for the rest ... of the ... summer."

"Deena, stay calm," I pleaded. "At least until we get your inhaler. You're making it worse." I shot Ty a look, asking for help.

"Anyway, I'd rather be locked in the house than out here with those guys," Ty said. "Unless it was your grandma's house, of course. Then I'd take my chances out here." Ty laughed, but Deena didn't even crack a smile.

We stood on the corner of Grandma's street. It was still and quiet. The sun had baked the life out of everything. The small patchwork lawns were brown, the leaves on the trees all drooped. A bunch of spilled Skittles melted together by the gutter. But we stood outside arguing. Ty refused to go in the front door.

"You don't have to come," Deena said, getting some of her breath back.

"What? And walk home by myself with those crazy guys out there somewhere? Okay, are you nuts?"

"Well, then, just come in," I argued. "Maybe she's taking an afternoon nap and you can sneak into the kitchen. She's not *that* bad."

"I can't deal with your grandma right now. Can't you let me in the basement? Please? It's not a big deal."

It's a good thing that Ty was so stubborn. If she hadn't been, who knows how long it would have been until we had found Eugene.

18

"Hey, Grandma." The cool air felt good, even if it did smell like sauerkraut and old socks. "Were you cooking?" I asked, crinkling my nose.

"No. That old Meals on Wheels crap came again." Grandma was sitting in her chair by the window, fingering her rosary beads. They were special, too, like the plate, and had been given to her by her mother when she made her First Communion. Each of the five large Our Father beads had three sides with pictures of the mysteries on them. Turn it one way and there is Jesus, a baby lying in the manger. Turn it another way and He is being crowned with thorns. On the third side, the Holy Spirit is hovering, in little balls of fire, over the heads of the disciples. I loved to look at those tiny pictures. I wanted the Holy Spirit to come down over me in a ball of fire, but Grandma explained that it didn't really work that way.

We don't go to church much anymore since Mom left. She was the one who made us get up early every Sunday and who took us to our religion classes. It seemed important back then, but we kind of got out of the habit after a while. At first, we prayed real hard that she would come back, but when she didn't come, I prayed less and less. I couldn't help it. It seemed like my words were floating in empty space and no one was catching them. Dad prefers to read the paper and drink his coffee on Sunday mornings and Deena and I never complain about it. We *could* walk to Mass by ourselves. But I like sitting on the couch with Dad better. He lets me have the sports page.

I still think about the Holy Spirit, though, and that ball of fire. I wish it could fall right from the sky and fill me up like it does to those disciples on the rosary bead. They got strong and brave and spent the rest of their lives doing good things. I'm not special enough or smart enough to change the world or anything. But I wonder if I went back to classes and made my confirmation if the Holy Spirit could make me strong and help me to figure out those things that I am always back and forth over in my head a hundred times.

Of course, maybe my parents were Jewish or Muslim or something like that and I shouldn't even believe in the Holy Spirit. But faith isn't in your genes. It's in your heart. And that's another problem. You are supposed to clean your heart to prepare for the Holy Spirit's visit on your confirmation day the way you are supposed to clean your house when company is coming. But I don't think my heart could ever get clean enough for the Holy Spirit. There are black spots in there that won't ever come out.

One day when Grandma wasn't looking, I put her rosary around my neck to see what it would look like as a necklace. Not only was it sparkly, but it made me feel kind of holy with its cross and all those pictures of Jesus. I was twirling in front of the mirror in her bedroom when she found me. She pulled the rosary over my head and quickly sprinkled it with the holy water that she keeps on her shelf next to the statue of the Blessed Mother. Then she placed it around the perfect, smooth blue plaster neck of Mary. It looked a lot better there than it did on me. I liked that Mary statue. Her face was always kind and she looked at me even then without any anger for what I had done. Grandma fished through her jewelry box and picked out a colorful necklace for me to keep. She never yelled at me, but she didn't let me hold the rosary ever again.

"Did you eat the Meals on Wheels?" Deena asked, plopping onto the couch.

"I ate some. The lady who brought it was colored, but she was real nice."

I sighed loudly. I was glad that Ty hadn't come in the front door. "I'm going to start the laundry, Grandma."

Deena jumped up. "I'll do the laundry!" Her face was flushed.

"No," I answered. "I'm doing it. Besides, you need to breathe in the air conditioning for a while. Then you can come help me fold."

"But it's cool in the basement and I ..."

Bang, bang, bang. Something was slamming against the back door. I looked at Deena. What was Ty doing? We only just got inside. I had told her I would come down in a minute to open the door.

"Oh, my heart!" Grandma squealed. "Someone's trying to

get in! Robbers. It's probably robbers!" She clutched the rosary to her chest. "They got into Emma Peterson's last week. Oh!"

Bang! Bang! Bang! The pounding was even louder this time.

I took off for the basement stairs. "Stay with Grandma, Deena!" I yelled.

"Come back here, Macey!" Grandma called, but I was already halfway down the steps.

Ty's face through the window was stricken. All I could think of were those creepy guys. We never should have left her alone. I fumbled with the key and pulled back the chain locks and the bolts. I threw the door open. I thought Ty wanted to get in, but she didn't. She pulled me out into the little cave-like entranceway and I almost tripped over him. Eugene was on his back on the ground. His skin was a weird color. His eyes were closed.

Ty was shaking. This wasn't anything we could handle. I knew that right away. I turned to her. "Call 9-1-1," I said. "Hurry."

I dropped to the ground next to him. "Eugene," I pleaded. "Eugene, what's the matter? Can you hear me?"

I held his hand. His eyes fluttered open and he stared at me, but he couldn't talk. He was trying. His blue lips moved a little, but nothing came out. I hoped that he wouldn't be mad at me for calling 9-1-1, but I was scared. I started to worry that I did something wrong. They would probably make him go back to Florida now and he really didn't want to do that.

"It's all right," I whispered, leaning close to him. "It's going to be okay." I believed it when I said it. Ty was calling 9-1-1. An ambulance would come. They would take him to the hospital and make him better. Maybe he had asthma, too, and couldn't get enough oxygen in this heat. The doctors would make him better. We could work out the Florida thing later.

A siren grew in the distance. Ty and Deena stood, flattened against the wall, watching. When the siren stopped out front, Ty ran to tell them to drive into the alley. Tires squealed around the corner. Heavy doors slammed. The stretcher clicked open as the EMTs pulled it from the ambulance, and keys jangled as they hustled to Eugene. He kept his eyes on me the whole time and I never looked away. I wish I knew what he was trying to tell me. Eugene squeezed my hand just before the ambulance guys moved me out of the way.

Their walkie-talkies squawked and they shouted instructions to each other. A crowd of curious neighbors gathered and stood around the humming ambulance.

"Where are this boy's parents?" the woman EMT called out to the onlookers as she helped the stretcher into the back of the van.

"Florida," I managed to say. "His mother's in Florida."

The woman said something under her breath, then jumped in behind Eugene. The ambulance driver turned on the siren and they sped away.

I wanted to go home, but Grandma wouldn't let us. She sat us on the couch and made us each drink a glass of lemonade that she made. She called Dad at work and told him that he had to come. I was worried that he might get in trouble and lose his job or something, and I tried to stop her. But Grandma said that this was important and he would want to be with us.

Deena and Ty were both crying. I don't know why, but I wasn't. I held the glass in my hand and took a small sip whenever Grandma ordered me to. Little flakes of dried milk floated in the lemonade. I didn't even care.

"Do you think he'll be okay?" Ty asked, blowing her nose into a hanky that Grandma had just put in her lap.

"Don't you worry, sweetie," Grandma consoled her. "Philadelphia has the best hospitals and doctors anywhere. They'll take good care of him."

I thought Grandma was going to launch into a story about her gall bladder surgery or her kidney stones, but she didn't.

In a half hour or so Dad burst through the door, still dirty from work. There was grease on his shirt and in the creases on his forehead. He took in the three of us on the couch in one quick glance, then pulled Deena up into his arms. He bent down and gave Grandma a quick kiss on the cheek. "Thanks, Mom."

"Call me," she said, leaning on her walker.

"I will. Let's go, girls."

Dad gave me a look. It lasted only a second, but it felt as though his eyes bored right into me and saw all the secrets that I had been hiding. I thought I could trust you, his expression said.

Ty and I got into the back seat and Dad kept Deena up front next to him. I sat as still as a statue, my insides all dry and cracked. It was only a few blocks to Ty's house. Dad kept the car running in the middle of the street with the air-conditioner blasting.

"C'mon, Ty," he urged. "Let's make sure your mom is home." He sprinted up the front steps, two or three at a time, and rapped on the front door. Ty's mom stepped out onto the stoop and I saw her head nodding up and down, and then she folded Ty into her arms.

Back in the car, Dad said little. I knew where we were going before Deena did. I could hear her breathing. She was taking quick panting breaths, like an exhausted dog. Her lungs were filling with fluid and she could get only a little air in at a time. Dad drove up to the emergency entrance of the hospital and rushed inside, carrying Deena in his arms.

I'd been here before. I knew the routine. There was nothing for the healthy kid to do but wait. And now that Mom was gone, there was no second parent to sit with me and assure me that everything would be fine. With no one to talk to, worry and guilt crept into the car and kept me company. If only I had been honest with Dad. I'm supposed to watch out for Deena and I didn't. And I did nothing but bring trouble to Eugene. I slumped in my seat and stared at the brick wall of the hospital until I began to feel dizzy from the heat. The inside of the car was like a sauna. I peeled my legs off the sticky seat and opened the door. The parking lot was baking and eerily quiet for a hospital. All the trees lining the driveway drooped, their leaves hanging deathly still. Even the birds sat silently in their nests. There was not a peep or a chirp anywhere. I hated to be inside hospitals, but I finally wandered toward the waiting room. The automatic doors shushed open and the blast of cool air made my skin tingle. The stale mediciney smell was worse than the sauerkraut at Grandma's. I picked a chair in the corner.

As soon as I sat down, it hit me that Mom might come back home if Deena were real sick. A thrill of hope flashed through me. What a horrible thing to think, to be excited about! But there it was and I couldn't stop it. It just popped into my head and I hated myself. I'm pretty sure that good people don't have horrible thoughts pop into their heads all the time. I didn't really want Deena to be seriously sick. I wanted her to be fine. I wanted her asthma to be cured and her health to be perfect, like the rest of her. So where did that thought come from? That's what worries me. It had to be inside me somewhere.

I wondered about my birth parents. Maybe they were evil. Maybe they committed awful crimes like murders or stabbings. If they did, that blackness could be in my genes, rumbling around deep inside of me, too deep to ever get out. My parents tried hard to raise me to be a good person, but what if the good part is just the outside coating, covering up my rotten core? And suddenly, with a sinking feeling, I was sure of it. How long would it be till the bad part came to the surface? I wanted to know what my parents did wrong so that I knew what to expect. Deena couldn't escape from Mom's asthma gene, and I saw little hope for my escape from the badness in my blood.

I sat for what felt like hours and stared at the scuffed linoleum between my feet. The waiting room was busy. Babies cried, moms and dads comforted children, husbands sat with their wives. People with arms in slings or swollen feet propped on chairs stared blankly at the television that droned above my head.

Dad finally came out and crouched in front of me. "You okay, baby?" he asked, patting my leg.

I nodded, but I couldn't look at him.

"I'm sorry it took so long. I couldn't get out here any earlier, Mace. Her oxygen count is really low. They had to give her a shot of adrenalin for her heart. But they've got a mask on her and she's going to be okay. She has to stay in the hospital, though."

"I should've noticed, Dad." I hung my head. "She was running and she shouldn't have and I didn't ..."

Dad took my face in his hands. "Hey," he interrupted. "Look at me."

But I couldn't.

"Macey, you didn't do anything wrong. There's nothing to feel bad about. C'mon, now."

But he didn't know. He was too good to know what I was really like. I wanted to ask him about my parents right that very second, to warn him about what was happening to me. It was burning in my throat and I blinked back the tears that sprung to my eyes.

Dad put some money in my hand. "Why don't you get a drink or some snacks out of the machine? After they get her all settled and she's calm, I'll come back for you. Okay? Are you okay?"

I nodded. I swallowed the burning down in my stomach.

"I can call Aunt Kate if you want. I'm sure she'd come for you."

"No, I'm good, really." I wanted to be alone anyway. "Dad?" I asked. "What about Eugene? How is he doing?"

"I don't know, Macey. He's not back in emergency. At least, I didn't see him. They probably took him to another hospital. After we get through all of this," he waved his arm around the stale waiting room, "maybe I can try to call his aunt for you and find out." He pulled me to him and hugged me hard. I felt how worried he was in the grip of his hands.

And then another bad thing came into my head uninvited. I suddenly wished that I was the one who was sick and he was worried about me, fussing over my bed, smoothing back my hair. I wished that Deena was sitting alone in the waiting room in a green plastic chair, that she was adopted and I was the real daughter, with history and roots and Dad's genes swimming through my blood. I would know who I was and where I came from. I would know what I was going to be. I'd trade my good lungs for that in a flash. Everyone is always feeling sorry for Deena because she has asthma. But she's the lucky one. It was wrong and it was ugly, but there it was. I couldn't turn those thoughts off. I couldn't stop them from coming. I had to find out who my birth parents were so I could know exactly how bad this was all going to get.

I was so focused on me. I didn't tell Dad that Eugene's aunt wasn't by his side at the hospital. No one was.

19

A commercial on TV says *Life comes at you fast.* I've been thinking that that was what happened to me. Month after boring month, there was nothing but school and homework and TV. And sure, I thought about Mom a lot, but that was just thinking. Then, in just a couple of days, everything happened. There was Eugene, the fight with Zach, the creepy guys at the bus stop and the deli, and Deena being sick. I felt like one of those circus jugglers with ten heavy things up in the air, concentrating so hard on keeping it all together. And then in one quick second I blinked and everything fell.

Dad brought me up to Deena's room to see her before we left. She looked so tiny in the hospital bed, with wires attached to her hand and a mask over her face. She was asleep, her head tilted to the side on the flat pillow, her damp hair spread out like a fan behind her. Dad was a nervous wreck, fiddling with the blankets, checking the monitors, straightening out the IV tube. Looking at the two of them made me feel guiltier than ever. They look so much alike, same perfect blue eyes and soft blond hair. They both have double-jointed thumbs and slightly crooked smiles.

Dad rested his hand on the side of Deena's face and stared down at her. I had to sit. And I wished it again, that my lungs were bad and not my heart.

"She's going to be fine," a skinny nurse said, cuffing Deena's arm and taking her blood pressure while she slept. "She'll be asleep for a while if you two want to go out and get a bite to eat." She gave Dad a big smile and I saw her eyes sweep over his face and down to his fingers. He doesn't wear his ring to work because it would get all greasy, and it was missing now. I jumped up and slipped my hand into his.

"You're sure?" Dad asked.

"I'm sure. We'll call you right away if she needs you."

Dad leaned over and kissed Deena's forehead.

"You hungry?" he asked as we rode down in the elevator, squeezed between the wall and a stretcher.

I shook my head.

"Well, if she's not, I am," said the man on the stretcher, laughing. He patted the IV bag hanging above his head. "After three days of this stuff, I'm up for anything. Bring me back a cheesesteak, would you?"

Before we reached the lobby, Dad and the patient figured out that they had about four friends in common and Dad had promised to take him out for a beer and a sandwich when he was well.

"This is my daughter, Macey." Dad put his hand on my shoulder.

"Pleased to meet you," the man said. His eyes jumped from Dad to me and back again. Maybe if Dad started introducing me as his adopted daughter, Macey, people wouldn't need to take that extra look or two at my skin and my face trying to figure out what was wrong. I don't match because I'm adopted. I should have it tattooed on my forehead. The elevator doors swished open.

I followed Dad through the lobby and into the parking lot. A pickup truck honked and someone called out to Dad. He went over and leaned against the driver's door, his arms resting on the open window. Deena usually gets frustrated because it takes us so long to get anywhere with the way that Dad always stops and talks to everyone. But I love to hear the sound of his voice and it was a comfort today, especially, to hear him laughing.

"Sorry, Mace," he apologized, opening the car door for me. "An old friend."

"I don't mind." I slipped into the front seat, taking Deena's spot.

He let the car idle for a minute with the air-conditioner blasting. It seemed like he was gathering his thoughts to say something to me, but he didn't. But then again, maybe he was waiting for me to explain things to him. I wasn't ready, though. There was too much to say and I couldn't figure out where to start. I needed time to think. Dad pulled out of the lot and we drove in silence until he turned into the McDonald's drive-through lane.

"But I'm not hungry," I complained. "And besides ..."

"You will be. You have to eat something, Mace. And don't worry. Mom wouldn't mind. It's okay to break the rules once in a while, right?"

"I guess." Mom never let us eat fast food because it was bad for our health. She said that it was disgusting. I always knew, though, that Dad used to sneak out and eat it sometimes. Every now and then when he kissed me good night, I could smell the Big Mac and fries on his breath, even though he tried to hide it by sucking peppermints. I wonder if Mom knew, too.

He placed the warm bag on the seat between us. We were both quiet, and I didn't even say anything when I noticed that we weren't headed for home. He only looked at me and winked as we turned onto Linden Avenue and drove straight for the river.

"I thought we could use a picnic," he said, grabbing the McDonald's bag.

Linden Avenue isn't the place that most people would consider a good picnic spot. Mainly, it's a boat-access ramp to the Delaware River and a big parking lot. But Deena and I always loved to climb over the rocks and skip stones into the water here.

Dad took off his work shirt and spread it on a small patch of dirt just short of the rocks. "Well, it's not a blanket, I know," he said, "but it's better than nothing. Have a seat."

When Mom was around, sometimes we would go all the way down to the Schuylkill River in Fairmount Park and picnic on the grass. She would bring the big basket with the red-checked napkins and we would eat chicken and potato salad and drink apple juice out of fluted glasses. Afterward we would go into the art museum, which was okay. Mostly I liked to run up the steps like Rocky did in the movie. So did Dad. But Mom asked us not to. Deena couldn't keep up and it wasn't good for her. It made her feel bad to be left behind. I didn't feel bad when I watched Deena at the district spelling bee or at Reading Olympics competitions. I don't know why she would feel bad watching me run up some steps.

Dad agreed with Mom, but he winked at me. The next time we were there, he said he got a cramp in his leg and told us to go on inside without him. But as I turned to leave, he tugged my shirt and, without a word between us, I knew what he was up to. I stayed behind with him and we ran the steps, dancing around at the top like Rocky, our fists pumping the air.

This was the Delaware, not the Schuylkill, and even though there was no grass or museum steps, it was still nice. I like being near the water. A few boats motored past us and an occasional Jet Skier, too.

I bit into my cheeseburger, but I didn't get to swallow because that's when Dad spoke up.

"You've been awfully quiet lately," he said. "Is there anything you want to tell me?"

It seemed like a pretty innocent thing to say. Maybe it was his voice or the way he asked the question. I don't know. I suppose I was holding a lot of stuff back, like one of those levees in New Orleans. His question poked a hole through and everything inside me just burst. I started to cry without warning. I surprised even myself. And I couldn't stop.

"Oh, Mace," Dad said, dropping his burger and putting his arm around me. "She's going to be okay. Don't worry."

I knew Deena was going to be okay. It was me I was worried about.

"We'll go back and visit after our picnic. Okay? She'll probably be awake by then and you can talk to her."

It's a good thing we had taken a stack of napkins from the McDonald's. I blew my nose into one and grabbed another to press against my leaky eyes. "It's not that," I sniffed.

"Well, what is it, Mace? You know you can talk to me."

Usually I could, but this was different.

"It's ... I don't know. ... It's ..." The question was right there in my throat, but I didn't know how to ask it.

Dad rested his arms on his knees and stared out at the river, waiting.

"My parents," I finally blurted. "My birth parents. Were they bad people? You know, I mean, did they commit crimes or anything? Because sometimes, sometimes I feel ..." I couldn't finish. It was too humiliating. I put the napkin over my face.

A pickup pulled in behind us, its wheels crunching over gravel. A few men in work clothes got out, jingling keys and joking with each other. They rustled through some tools in the bed of the truck, then headed toward the small restaurant that sat to our left on the water's edge.

Dad was stiff and silent. I waited, but even after those guys were gone, he didn't say anything. Nothing. Not one word. So it was true. My worst fears were true. There was a monster inside me.

I tried to look at him, but his face was a blank. He just sat there and stared into space. I jumped up and ran down to the water. I couldn't stand to see him so still, so hard.

"Mace, wait!" he called. "Come back."

But I didn't. I ran faster. Thief. Murderer. Bank robber. Drug dealer. I could be any one. And no matter how far I ran, I couldn't get away. It was inside me. I wanted to run for miles, for days, but I immediately came to a dead end. The deck from the restaurant jutted out over the water and a wooden fence ran the length of it. It didn't used to be here. I curled my fingers through the slats. I should have run the other way, up Linden Avenue. Peanut shells and lost straws lapped up against the rocks below me. Unless I wanted to swim, I had to go back to the parking lot. Dad knew that. He stood there waiting for me.

"Mace!" Dad yelled again. "Please come back." But he didn't follow me. He only waited.

Did he ever wonder when my parents' bad genes would begin to show in me? Did Mom? When I forgot the multiplication tables and yawned during the tours of the art museum, did she see the trouble beginning? She tried so hard to make me fit into our family, but the task was impossible. My genes were set the moment I was born. It would have made so much more sense if I had been the one to run away. I watched the river. It was the same dirty brown as my skin, with the same trash floating below the surface. All it takes is a good storm to bring it up—the tires and old milk crates, abandoned shoes, and soggy boxes. Maybe my storm was happening now. I had wished that Zach would die. I was jealous of Deena, with her perfect hair and her straight A's and even her bad lungs that got her so much attention. And even though I kept trying to push it down, this anger toward Mom kept rising up inside me. Sometimes, I thought I hated her.

What would Dad do when he realized what kind of person I was? I turned to look at him. His hands were shoved deep in his pockets and his shoulders were bent. He stood there staring at me. No matter what, it wasn't fair of me to hurt him. He didn't deserve it. I climbed back over the rocks to the parking lot. He pulled me to him and hugged me hard. But still, he didn't say anything. He just held me.

When he finally pulled away, I saw something I had never seen before in my entire life. He was crying. He pressed his hands to his eyes for a second, then gave me a small smile.

"Let's get out of here," he said.

We threw away all our uneaten food and got into the car.

He turned to face me. "Mace, about your question …," he began.

"It's all right," I quickly interrupted, "you don't have to answer." His silence had been all the answer that I needed anyway. I was scared to hear the particulars about what kind of evil swam through my blood. I didn't feel like I could take it right now.

"No. I do have to answer. You just surprised me. I wasn't ready. And, you know, I always imagined that Mom would be here to help me out." He ran his hands through his hair. "I'm not too good at this stuff."

"Really, Dad, you don't have to tell me. Let's just go."

"No, Macey, you deserve an answer. If I were you, I'd want

to know. But I have to warn you that it's not a good story, and you have to be ready for it."

"So my parents were criminals?"

"No! Why would you think that? They weren't criminals. To tell the truth, I don't know anything about your father. But your mother was only fifteen years old when she gave birth. She wasn't a bad person, Mace. She was young and scared and she didn't know what to do."

"That's it?" I asked. "She was scared and she just gave me up?"

He paused. "She left you, Mace."

"Left me where?"

He looked down at his hands. "In a bag."

"Like ... like a trash bag?"

Dad nodded.

"She didn't leave me at a hospital or police station or something?" A panic was growing in my stomach.

"She left you out by the street. I'm so sorry, Macey." He put his arm around my shoulder. "But it has nothing to do with *you* or who *you* are. She was just young and scared. She didn't think she had anybody to turn to." He paused for a deep breath. "But Macey, if it hadn't ever happened, I wouldn't have you. And I just can't imagine that."

"She put me in the trash? My own mother put me in the trash!" It was worse than I thought. I wished she had robbed a bank instead.

"Oh, Macey, don't think of it that way." Dad put his arms around me and held me.

But I pulled away. What other way was there to think of it? I held up my hand. "My thumb?" I asked.

"It was winter," Dad said. "It was very cold. By the time someone found you, you had frostbite. They had to take it off." He winced. "I'm sorry, Macey. I'm so sorry that that happened to you. I can't even bear to think of it."

I rubbed the empty space where my thumb used to be. Somehow it was better to think of it as never having been there. To have had a thumb and then lost it, that was worse. I wonder what they did with it after they took it off.

Music suddenly filled the car. "Sorry," Dad said, unclipping his cell phone from his belt. "It's the hospital. I have to take it. Hello?"

I didn't even listen. How can I ever explain what it feels like to learn that your own mother threw you in the trash? That you were so worthless and so unwanted that you sat at the curb with rotting food and broken bicycles. It's like a punch in the stomach from a giant fist and all the air goes out of your body. You're numb and you hurt at the same time.

"She's awake," Dad said, clipping the phone back to his belt. "She's asking for us."

"Can I just walk home?" I asked.

"Walk? Macey, our house is miles from here."

That was what I wanted, though. A long, long walk. I didn't care how long it took. I hopped out of the car.

"Macey!" Dad followed me.

"Go," I said. "Deena's awake. You should be with her. I'll be fine."

Dad came around the car and grabbed my arm. "Just a minute," he said. "Just wait, okay?" He was pacing back and forth in front of the car, wringing his hands, his eyes on the ground. "Macey," he said, finally looking up at me. "I love Deena. You know that, right? I love her just as much as you. And I'm not saying that I could ever have a favorite daughter or anything like that because you're both wonderful. Deena, she looks just like me, doesn't she? But Macey, you ..." He stopped pacing and stood right in front of me, his hand over his heart. "Macey, you and me, we're the same in here." He patted his hand on his chest. "And I don't know what I would ever do without that."

And all at once I knew he was right. How many times had he caught my eye and told me something without saying a word? How many times had he figured out what was bothering me before I had a chance to tell him? Hadn't I always felt that connection? Where did it come from? We didn't have the same genes. Maybe there was something else, something you could inherit just from living with a person, just from loving them year after year.

His phone rang again. "I'm so sorry, Macey. I wish I could turn it off." He looked down at the number.

"The hospital again?" I asked.

He nodded.

I didn't want be alone anymore. I wanted to be with him. "Can I come?"

A smile spread across his face. "Let's go."

We jumped back in the car and headed for the hospital.

Dad was focused on getting through the traffic. I kept stealing glances at him and he looked over once and smiled at me with Deena's crooked smile. I couldn't stop thinking about genes. They had everything to do with how you looked, from the color of your hair to the shape of your nose. But maybe they didn't matter so much on the inside. After all, Dad isn't anything like Grandma, and Ryan is one thousand times nicer than Zach. Why hadn't I thought about that before? A feeling of relief washed through me, cool and wonderful. Maybe I wasn't doomed by my genes, destined to turn out like my birth parents.

"You know," I said finally as we turned onto the boulevard, "some things have happened that I haven't told you about." I gave him the whole story of the creepy guy at our house, the men at the deli, and all about Eugene.

Dad listened in silence till the end, his knuckles glowing white as he gripped the steering wheel. He glanced away from the traffic for a second to look at me. "You're telling me that Eugene has no parents or anyone else with him right now while he's in the hospital?"

"Probably not."

Dad moved into the left lane and began to speed.

20

When we finally found Eugene, it was too late. He had died shortly after they got him to the hospital. No one knew who he was. No one was with him.

In a small office outside the emergency room, I told everything I knew to a police officer and a lady social worker. Dad sat beside me. It was strange, but I didn't cry. I was having a hard time feeling anything at all, except guilt. My mind whirled with thoughts of what I could have done differently. If I had told Dad everything right away, about the locket, the creepy guys, about Eugene being alone, it would have all turned out differently. Just an hour ago I was feeling good about my talk with Dad, but once again I was thinking only of myself. Eugene would have been better off if he had never met me. It didn't seem real that he was dead.

The police eventually found Eugene's aunt and she had to go identify him. It turns out that she was really his great aunt, as old as my grandmother, and lived in an assisted-living facility. Even if we had found her, there wouldn't have been room for Eugene. The worst part was that his mother and stepfather didn't come to the funeral. I don't know why.

I'm still not even sure why Eugene died. Dad said that it had something to do with a heart defect. Even though I didn't know him that long, I think Eugene had a good heart and the people around him had the defects. I'll never know why he ran away. Dad says that you can't tell what goes on inside people's houses. Maybe Eugene had a good reason for running away, but maybe he was mistaken. It all depends on the way you look at a situation. I'm sure Mom felt like she had a good reason for running away. But even though I lived in the same house with her, I can't see it. I have to try every day not to feel angry with her. And lots of days, I fail. How could she do such a thing to us?

I go over and over in my head the times that I let Mom down. I wasn't smart enough or careful enough or neat enough all the time. But I'm not Deena and I never will be. What did I ever do that was so wrong that she had to leave? Nothing. That's what makes me mad.

I've thought about my time with Eugene, too. Maybe I should have listened to him better, and I know I made a lot of mistakes with all the stuff that happened. But I like to think that at least I was a good friend to him those last couple of days. I stood up to Zach, I helped Eugene with a place to sleep, and I promised to help find his aunt. We held hands in the dark. Even though I still worry about the ugly black thoughts that grab hold of me at times, I know there's good in me, too. After all, I've realized that I do take after Dad in some ways, at least on the inside. That's what I'm going to focus on.

I wish I could turn back time and have a do-over for

certain things. Dad says that's normal, and he thinks there are about a million moments in his past that he would want to do over again. He didn't mention Mom, but I know that's what he was thinking about.

Eugene saved our lives that day. Somebody called 9-1-1 when we were trapped behind the deli with those crazy guys. It could have been a neighbor looking out a window, but I'm pretty sure it was Eugene. He was even smarter than Deena. He ran when he could and called for help. Who knows what would have happened to us if he hadn't? Maybe that guy would have used that knife he was pointing at us. He was sure mad about us not having any money. People have been killed for far less in Philadelphia.

Eugene's aunt, Mrs. Wilson, didn't have money for the funeral. I listened in when Dad was on the phone with her. I didn't even feel bad about that. I figured after all Eugene and I had been through together, I had a right to know what she was saying. Her voice wasn't shaky, like Grandma's. It was calm and nice, but she did sigh into the receiver a lot. She used to be a teacher at Lincoln High School in Mayfair. Dad managed to find six people that they knew in common. Mrs. Wilson was laughing by the end of the conversation, even though she was sad that Eugene's mother wouldn't be coming to the funeral. The church helped out with the cost and so did Dad. Deena and I agreed to do the readings. Ty was going to bring up the gifts. I guess she did, but that part of the Mass came after I had already left.

I pulled the necklace out of the small pocket on the front

of my dress. I still carry it around even though I wish I had never found it.

When I looked up, I saw Dad in his dark suit, walking quickly down the block toward home. When he got to our house, he climbed the cement steps and sat beside me. He didn't say anything, he just kept me company. He fussed for a while with a loose thread on the lapel of his jacket, then rested his arms on his knees.

"Is it over, then?" I finally asked.

"Almost. Deena said you left early. I got there a little late."

I looked down at the ground. "I didn't feel good." I still had that terrible taste of throw-up in the back of my mouth. I wished I had cried instead of vomited. That would have been more normal.

I wonder if my feelings will sort themselves out when I grow up or if I will always be this messed up. I could live to be one hundred and I don't think that I'd ever be able to sort out my feelings and neatly separate them, like the papers in Mom's organized file folders. I can be so angry at her one minute and ache to have her home the very next second. I am jealous of Deena sometimes but also so happy for her when she wins her awards. Maybe that's not too weird. Dad loves Grandma even when she drives him crazy.

"I know," Dad said. "I don't do good at funerals either."

"Is Deena mad?" I asked.

"She's not mad. She was worried about you. I told her that I'd find you." Dad loosened his tie and unbuttoned the collar of his shirt. "What do you have there, the locket?"

I opened my hand wide and showed him. "Yeah. I don't want it anymore." I dropped it into his palm.

Dad raised his eyebrows at me.

"I was wrong. Mom didn't leave it for me." I lowered my voice. "And I know she's not coming back." I had thought it before, but saying it out loud gave me an actual physical pain in my chest.

Dad sighed. "You know, Mace, how you felt real bad about not telling me everything that happened with Eugene and those guys?"

"Yeah."

"Well ..." He turned to face me. "I haven't told you and Deena everything either. I meant to. It's just that I kept hoping that there wouldn't be anything to tell. I thought that everything would get fixed and turn out okay, you know? I guess I sort of believed in magic lockets, too." He bent his head and ran both his hands back through his hair. The edges above his ear were turning dark with perspiration. "I'll tell you one thing I do know. Mom really meant to come back. You can't be mad at her. She's so smart, Macey, much smarter than me, and she had lots of plans that she put on hold for us. And she's kind of high-strung. She had a problem with her nerves sometimes. When she was out visiting her sister, she had a nervous breakdown."

I pictured Mom shaking and broken. "We should have visited her." I cried. "Why didn't we help her, Dad? We could have brought her home!"

Dad shook his head. "I didn't know about it till too late.

And it's more complicated than you think, Mace. She was in a treatment facility, kind of like a hospital, and when she was discharged, she went off somewhere. I'm not sure where she is right now. Your mom might just need some time to figure things out."

"Like what? What could she have to figure out? Couldn't she at least call us to let us know?" I couldn't say that I understood, because I didn't. I felt sorry for Mom and I loved her, but I was mad at her, too, all at the same time. It seemed so mean of her to leave us wondering and worrying this way.

Dad sighed. "Well, think of it this way. What happened to Mom was like an injury. If you broke your leg, you couldn't get up and start walking right away. It takes time to heal. Mom's injury takes time to heal, too."

I broke my leg once when I was in second grade. The cast came off after six weeks. Mom has been gone almost a full year.

Dad must have read my mind, but it sounded like he was talking to himself. "I don't know how long it takes. I don't know."

I took the locket back from Dad. "I wish I had never found this," I said. "I hate it. I don't know why I pretended it was from Mom."

"It's okay. Sometimes we need to dream about what we want. That's all you did."

I squeezed it in the palm of my hand, feeling the edge of the heart cut into my palm. "No. It's not just that. It started all the trouble."

"C'mon, how could a locket start trouble?"

"Because I found it and I wouldn't show it to Deena because I knew she would tell me that it had nothing to do with Mom, and I wanted to think that it did. Deena thought I had found money and I was hiding it and she got mad at me. Then that creepy guy was waiting for the bus and he wanted it."

"The locket?"

"I thought that's what he wanted."

Dad sat up straight. "What did he look like?" he asked. "Tell me again."

I described his yellow eyes, long stringy hair, and hollowed-out face.

Dad stood up. "Had you seen him around here before?"

"Yeah. Standing down there, by the wall, waiting for the bus. I saw him a bunch of times. It was that guy you read about in the newspaper who got beaten up on Rockland Street."

"Wait there." Dad hurried into the house and came out with a metal pick. He started to bang away at the mortar between the stones in the wall.

"What are you doing?"

"I don't know. I might be crazy, but I have a hunch."

Dad took off his suit jacket and shirt and handed them to me. I ran them into the house. He didn't care that his pants and good shoes were getting all flecked with mortar and dust. I stood behind him and watched. The bus squealed to a stop and a few passengers got off, including George P., his lunch box in his hand.

Dad was so intent on the wall, he didn't notice right away. "Hey, George P.! How you doing?" he asked. He put the pick down and showed his hands. "They're a little dirty," Dad said.

George P. nodded and smiled shyly. He and Dad have an elaborate hand-shaking ritual that they do whenever they meet. They were doing it now, and George P. laughed at the dust that was clouding above their arms with each slap. After they were done, he picked up his lunch box and headed home. He was staring at his hands as he walked.

Dad went back to work. When the first stone was loose enough, he inched it out of the wall and dropped it on the sidewalk. He stuck his hand in the hole he had made, felt around, and then started on the next stone.

"Are you taking all the stones out?" I asked, worried about his sanity.

"Nope. Just the ones I fixed a week or so ago."

The next stone came out quicker. He stuck his hand in again, but deeper this time, his whole arm disappearing into the wall. He pulled out a bag. "Take this into the house, Macey, and wait for me in there. I'm just going to put these stones back."

I held a crumpled brown paper bag, about the size of a fat book. I walked it inside carefully, like it was an egg ready to hatch. It was covered in dust and dirt. I slowly placed it on the coffee table. A small red ant ran across the top and disappeared beneath the bag. With the very edges of my fingers I carefully lifted one end, peeking inside. I couldn't believe it. I held my breath till Dad came. He burst in the door and dropped the pick on the carpet. He lowered himself onto the couch, not caring that he was covered in a dusty gray film.

"It's money," I gasped.

He nodded. "I know. Let's see how much."

Dad slid the bills from the bag. I had never seen so much money before in my life. There must have been thousands of dollars there.

"How did you know?" I asked.

"I guessed. You know how those creeps sell drugs on the corners at Quinlan and Everly, the ones I make you stay away from? The guy you described used to hang out at Quinlan near the hardware store. The cops have been cracking down on them and chasing them away. I've seen him at our corner a lot recently. He wasn't selling that I could tell, but he wasn't waiting for the bus either. I wasn't thinking of that when I cemented those loose stones. He was using our wall as a drop spot. You know, put the drugs in, take the money out. I didn't make the connection before when you told the story to the police officer. It just struck me now. That guy thought that you took his money and were keeping it all to yourself."

"Oh! I get it now!" I gingerly touched the piles of bills. "So the locket had nothing to do with anything! But who were those other guys?"

"They must be the people he owed the money to. When he didn't pay, they beat him up. He must have told them that you had it."

The screen door slammed. Deena and Ty stood in front of us, their mouths open.

"We robbed a bank," I joked. It was all I could think of saying.

21

I had never been in a police station before. I guess most people haven't. It was interesting and scary at the same time. I kept thinking that this year in school when I have to write my personal narrative, I will finally have something to write about. There were a bunch of desks all jammed close together and people running back and forth between them. Radios squawked, phones rang. File cabinets were crammed into every available open space. The floor was so old that it was worn right through in certain places. A big window air-conditioner wasn't working too well. It clanked loudly every few minutes and the air coming out of it smelled like burnt rubber. It was blowing right in my face. On the other side of the room was a lady in jeans and old sneakers. She was hand-cuffed to a chair.

The detective must have been watching my face. "Shoplifting," he said with a jerk of his head, answering my unasked question.

He made me sit in the chair beside his desk. Dad stood behind me with his hands on my shoulders. Deena and Ty squeezed beside Dad.

"So let's figure out who you all are to start with, okay?" The detective had a pad and pen and waited for Dad to begin.

Dad gave our information.

"Wait a minute. This girl is your daughter, too?" he asked, pointing to me. He did the usual double take.

I felt Dad's hands tighten on my shoulders. "Yes, she is," he answered firmly. "I just said so, didn't I?"

"All right. Just checking I got everything right. Now what is it you want to file a complaint about?" The detective covered his mouth to stifle a large yawn.

"We're not filing a complaint. We came because of this." Dad plopped the bag of money right on top of the detective's pad.

Dad explained what happened about three times over before the detective seemed to understand. His hair was jet black and combed back from his forehead. He leaned back in his swivel chair and chewed on his pen.

"Hold on. I'll be right back," he said.

The shoplifter woman brought her shackled hands up to her mouth and chewed on her nails. She glared at me.

"What do you think he's doing?" Deena whispered.

"I don't know," Dad answered. "We'll have to wait and see."

A few minutes later, the detective appeared in the doorway across the room and motioned for us to follow him. We filed through the maze of desks and ended up in a small office.

A tall, heavy man with graying hair stood and shook Dad's hand. "I'm Captain Mitchell," he said. "Have a seat."

There were two chairs, but only Dad sat. The detective leaned against the wall, his head resting on a picture of the mayor. The bag of money was on the desk.

"You found this money on your property?" Captain Mitchell asked.

"Yes, we did. Hidden in the stone wall in front of our house," Dad replied.

"Well, what would you like us to do about it?"

Dad tried to explain what happened, but Captain Mitchell interrupted him.

"Listen, sir, I already know the story and we do appreciate that you're here trying to do the right thing. But all that happened is that you found some money. No one has claimed it. It was on your property. I have no evidence whatsoever that any crime was committed in relation to this money. There's nothing that I can do for you."

"Well, then, what am I supposed to do with it?" Dad asked.

"For a start, you could take these girls out for some ice cream." He winked at me. "After that, it's up to you."

"But it's not my money!" Dad insisted. "I don't want those drug dealers coming anywhere near my girls to look for it."

"I can understand your concern." Captain Mitchell opened a file on his desk and pulled out a paper. "But Mr. Delladonna, whom I believe Miss Macey here has met before, is not going to claim that money as his. He's being released from the hospital tomorrow into police custody. He's got a long list of priors, and there was a warrant out for his arrest for skipping his last hearing. You won't be seeing him for a while. We got IDs on the other two men, and they're also wanted on outstanding warrants. We'll have them picked up before too long. They will not be claiming that money as theirs. I can guarantee it."

Dad shook his head. "I don't know. It just doesn't feel right, somehow."

"Look, sir, this is not enough money to make anybody rich. There is no one to give it back to. You found it on your property. I'm sure you'll find something worthwhile to do with it."

"But, it's drug money," Dad protested.

"I have no way of connecting that money to a drug sale unless you witnessed a transaction. Did any of you see it happen?"

We all shook our heads.

"Well, then, there's nothing I can do. I'm sorry to kick you out, but I've got some matters here that need my attention. We will be in touch as soon as those two men are apprehended. Till then, keep the girls close to home and keep an eye on them. We do appreciate you coming in."

We took the captain's advice and bought ice cream at Mick's. We sat on the swings at the playground eating it, Ty and Deena, me and Dad. It was late afternoon and the ice cream dripped down our hands faster than we could lick it. We ran through the cool water that sprayed from the green dolphin's spout until we were soaked and our shoes squished with every step. We flew down the slide in our wet clothes, the metal burning hot right through our shorts, and swung across the rungs of the monkey bars, daring each other not to touch the ground. We saw Ryan and Zach, in their uniforms, headed toward a game. Ryan waved through the chain link fence, but Zach kept his eyes on the sidewalk. We hadn't played like this since we were much younger, and I don't know why we were doing it now. Dad sat on the bench and laughed at us. The space beside him seemed so empty, and I could still clearly picture Mom there.

I'm getting used to the idea that she's not coming back at any moment. She isn't hiding in a nearby apartment watching me and leaving small signs for me on the grass beside the step. I try to think how something must have broken inside her and how it takes longer to heal than an arm or a leg. Maybe she'll get better, but maybe she won't. Dad says it's not her fault, so I try not to be mad.

Dad showed me an envelope that he and Mom keep in a drawer in their bedroom. Inside were my adoption papers. I might want to find my birth mother someday to find out what she's like and why she did what she did to me. But I don't want to now and I may not ever. Dad and Deena are the best family a person could ask for. And Mom may have left, but she might be back. And she did love us. Dad is right about that.

I don't worry so much about my genes anymore. I've thought a lot about how Dad said that he and I have the same heart. It's true. We're connected in a way that is stronger than genes or blood. I may not have inherited his blue eyes or crooked smile, but I can take after him in a million other ways because I get to choose the kind of person I want to be. And I want to be like him.

Deena came up with a really good idea for some of the money. We bought two trees. We planted one in the courtyard at Mrs. Wilson's assisted-living home. A plaque on the ground underneath it says In Memory of Eugene, a Good Friend with a Kind Heart. Mrs. Wilson can sit outside on the bench there and watch Eugene's tree grow. Deena and I visit sometimes and Mrs. Wilson tells us stories of things Eugene did when he was a little boy. She even had pictures of Eugene that his father, her nephew, had sent to her in the years before he died. That is the way I will remember Eugene, smiling, with a fishing pole in his hand, leaning against his dad.

We planted the bigger tree on the small patch of ground out in front of our house. We didn't need a plaque. It will give us shade in the summer and flowers in the spring. The leaves turn bright red in the fall. Deena loves to read underneath it. I like to sit under the branches and watch the world go by on our street. Mom may not be here right now, but I like to think of it as her tree. We'll take care of it until she gets back. Until then, we've got each other.